It was time to
stop running....

Suddenly Ethan's  ng her face,
one thumb tentat[...]
of her lower lip[...]
hoarsely, and th[...]

"No!" She pushed he[...]
taking a few quick, unsteady st[...]
her eyes wide and wary.

He didn't move, and somehow Frances found
that more ominous than if he had tried to overpower her. He just stood there, bright strands
of blond hair quivering over his brow. His rain-
soaked T-shirt clung to his chest, outlining the
musculature that rose and fell rapidly with each
breath.

"Excuse me," Frances breathed, in panicked,
automatic politeness that was silly under the
circumstances. She moved quickly to push past
him, only to find herself spun around when his
hand snaked out to grasp her wrist.

"You're running away from yourself, Frannie,
not me."

MELINDA CROSS would love her readers to believe she was kidnapped as a child by an obscure nomadic tribe and rescued by a dashing adventurer. Actually, though, she is a wonderfully imaginative American writer who is married to a true romantic. Every spring, without fail, when the apple orchard blooms, her husband gathers a blanket, glasses and wine and leads Melinda out to enjoy the fragrant night air. Romantic fantasy? Nonsense, she says. This is the stuff of real life.

Books by Melinda Cross

Don't miss any of our special offers. Write to us at the following address for information on our newest releases.

Harlequin Reader Service
P.O. Box 1397, Buffalo, NY 14240
Canadian address: P.O. Box 603,
Fort Erie, Ont. L2A 5X3

MELINDA CROSS

Mirror Image

Harlequin Books

TORONTO • NEW YORK • LONDON
AMSTERDAM • PARIS • SYDNEY • HAMBURG
STOCKHOLM • ATHENS • TOKYO • MILAN
MADRID • WARSAW • BUDAPEST • AUCKLAND

Harlequin Presents first edition March 1993
ISBN 0-373-11535-0

Original hardcover edition published in 1991
by Mills & Boon Limited

MIRROR IMAGE

CHAPTER ONE

FRANCES folded the last silk shirt into the open suitcase lying on her bed, rearranging and smoothing the sleeves again and again. When she was satisfied that they wouldn't wrinkle she snapped the case closed, sighed, then turned to the full-length mirror to check her appearance one last time.

At first glance, her reflection always gave her a start. She still expected to see little Frannie Hudson in the mirror—a scrawny, scrappy, inner-city tomboy in hand-me-down dresses and red pigtails. Even though the outward evidence of that little girl had been gone for a long time, Frances still found herself looking for her in the mirror.

She eyed her reflection with critical objectivity, approving the conservative, executive image she had created. She'd learned long ago that image was everything—that people accepted the image you presented rather than taking the trouble to see the person beneath—and she'd been capitalizing on that piece of knowledge for years. The day she'd traded those hand-me-down dresses for the expensive suits of a rising young professional had been the day the business world had opened its arms to her, and she'd been on an upward climb ever since.

No one knew that the Frances Hudson who lived in this elegantly decorated town house had moved here directly from a cramped, shabby second-story walk-up; that the chic, sophisticated woman in the mirror was just a clever disguise for a fatherless tomboy from one of Boston's poorest neighborhoods—no one but her mother, of course. And there were times when even her mother barely recognized the woman her daughter had become.

The bright red pigtails of her youth had darkened with the years, and when she brushed her hair over her shoulders at night it resembled nothing as much as hot caramel melting over a crisp autumn apple—but no one ever saw that either. Today, as every day, it was pulled tightly against her head, captured and tamed in a rigid coil at the nape of her neck, a style as severe as the cut of the suits she wore. Normally she preferred rigid pinstripes and dark colors, but this morning's muggy air, unseasonably warm for early June had made her choose a lightweight linen in a butter-cream color.

She made a face at her eyes before turning from the mirror—the only feature that spoiled the image of a sophisticated woman in constant control. They were unmistakably catlike, such a light brown that at times they appeared almost amber, and there was a suggestion of something hot and wild behind them, something that didn't belong in proper society.

Men in particular backed away from whatever it was they saw in her eyes, and she had yet to encounter one who could meet her gaze for more than a few seconds at a time.

Before leaving on the business trip that might last as long as two weeks, Frances made a leisurely last tour of her town house. It was more an act of pleasure than of necessity. It was always a comfort to walk through the carefully decorated rooms, measuring her success by the things she had acquired. Most of the time she still felt like little pigtailed Frannie, trespassing in the elegant home of some stranger, awed by the polished antiques, the limited edition prints, the Aubusson rugs. She was almost perversely attached to these symbols of her achievements, as if they were the confirmation that the woman in the mirror actually existed.

Back in the bedroom she sat at the lacquered dressing table, careful to smooth her skirt beneath her first, and reached for the phone. Four miles away on the other side of Boston—light years and lifetimes away in a cramped second-floor apartment in a neighborhood of cramped second-floor apartments—a woman's voice answered.

"Hello, Mother—it's Frances. How are you?"

Her mother never told her how she was. She told her instead about Mrs. Booker next door and how her arthritis troubled her in the June heat, how cute that little Katy McFiel down the hall was getting, and did she know that old Mr. Winger had finally sold the corner butcher shop and retired to Florida? Always, she told her about the old neighborhood, when all Frances cared about was her. "So. How are you, Frannie?" her mother finally ended her recitation of news.

"I'm fine, Mother. I just wanted to let you know I'll be out of town for a week or so. I have a fire investigation up in New Hampshire."

"New Hampshire?" Some of the warmth left her mother's voice, as it always did when they discussed Frances's work. It wasn't that she wasn't proud of her daughter's steady, determined climb up the corporate ladder of Northeastern Casualty Insurance; she just didn't understand the point of it all. Why would any woman want a career when there were men to be married and children to be had?

"It's a big claim, Mother; the insured lost nearly half a million dollars in property in a fire of some sort last night. Usually they give a claim of this size to one of the men investigators."

"You should be dating those men, Frannie, not competing with them."

Frances rolled her eyes. "If I can prove it's a fraudulent claim and save the company the money, my bonus is seven percent—that's thirty-five thousand dollars, Mother." She enunciated each syllable of the staggering amount, but it was pointless. Money had never been her mother's measure of success.

"Well, if you're happy about the assignment, of course I'm happy for you, Frannie. It's just that sometimes I wish you'd chosen a profession where you didn't profit from other people's misfortunes."

It was hopeless. Her mother would never understand the insurance business, no matter how often she explained it. "Mom, it's not a misfortune when people destroy their own property just to collect the insurance money—it's a crime. It's my job to make sure that the claims filed are legitimate. That's what I do. That's what all insurance investigators do."

Her mother sighed. "Well, at least you'll be getting out of the city for a change. You be sure to give those people my sympathy for their loss."

"I will, Mother." Frances kept the smile out of her voice, amazed, as she always was, that a woman the world had treated so harshly still felt such empathy for others. "I'll call you when I get back, Mom. Take care of yourself."

"Frannie?"

She brought the receiver back to her ear. "Yes, Mom?"

"I *am* proud of you, you know."

"I know that, Mother."

"I just wish you were...happier."

"I am happy, Mom. I really am." Saying the words was like banging your head against the proverbial brick wall. Her mother would never believe she was happy without a man at her side and children at her feet.

She replaced the receiver with a sigh, feeling the disconnection on a much deeper level than simply the end of a phone conversation.

Less than an hour later she was in the black, expensive sedan she'd saved for four years to buy, driving very fast on the highway that stretched northwest from Boston to slice through the heart of New Hampshire. She barely noticed the lush green of the June landscape rolling past the ribbon of concrete. As far as Frances was concerned, country was simply a boring emptiness that connected the excitement of one city to another. Her dream had always been fixed on the glass and steel towers of downtown wealth. As a child she had sworn that one day she would escape the poor neighborhood of her youth, and now she had. Of course she was happy. Why couldn't her mother see that?

After two hours of travel on a nearly deserted highway, the exit sign for the town she was looking for suddenly loomed directly ahead. "Nowthen," it read, and Frances thought again that it was the silliest name for a town she'd ever heard.

She stopped at the top of the ramp and her lips formed a silent whistle at the empty countryside that met her glances to left and right. There wasn't a single sign of human habitation in either direction.

In the five years she'd worked for Northeastern Casualty, first as an assistant and then as a full-fledged certified investigator, her assignments had always been within the Boston metropolitan area. Being sent out in the field on her own was a feather in her career cap, certainly; but it was also a little disconcerting. She was a city girl, after all, not just by birth but by choice, and the sheer emptiness of the New Hampshire countryside intimidated her.

She felt like a pioneer, lost in a wilderness of forests and grasslands, and for the first time she thought that maybe packing her best designer suits and shoes hadn't been such a good idea. She had a sudden, nightmarish image of a farmer in overalls sitting on a sagging front porch, a loaded shotgun balanced on his knee, and she laughed nervously to dispel the picture. People like that didn't insure pieces of their personal property for half a million dollars, she consoled herself. Somewhere in this godforsaken no-man's-land there was an island of civilization, probably a country estate owned by some fabulously wealthy man who used it as a retreat from the bustle of the city. Now all she had to do was find the place.

The village of Nowthen was a full five miles from the highway, and she'd seen only a few scattered farms in that entire distance. It was a genuine relief to pull over the crest of a hill and see a bustling town below, complete with cars, trucks, paved streets—all the welcome signs of the twentieth century.

She stopped at the first gas station—the only one, she learned later—pulled up to the pumps, and smiled at the grizzled man who walked up to her window. He whisked the peaked cap from his balding head in a gesture of automatic respect she rarely saw in Boston.

"'Morning," he said, his tone a good deal less courtly than his gesture. "Gas?"

"Fill it, please," she said, a little amused by the quick, suspicious glance he gave her, then her car. Obviously she was overdressed *and* over mounted for this little town. "I'm looking for the Harmon place," she called out of the window, and, although he looked straight at her, he didn't say another word until he finished filling the tank, returned to her window, then counted the notes she'd given him as if he was convinced she had tried to cheat him.

He pocketed the notes and eyed her suspiciously. "Franklin know you're comin'?" His tone stated what his words had left unsaid—if Franklin Harmon *didn't* know she was coming, there was no way in the world she'd get directions out of this man. Either he was a close personal friend of the Harmons, or Nowthen was a town as tightly knit as a small family.

"I'm sure he does."

"Ah." A hundred wrinkles carved a smile in his weathered face. "Well, if you're a friend of Franklin's, you're surely welcome in Nowthen." He jammed a grease-blackened hand in through the window, and Frances had no choice but to take it and shake it gingerly. "You just keep goin' on this road about another five miles, and watch for a long drive lined with elms once you cross the creek. That's Franklin's place."

Frances thanked him politely and pulled out of the station, resisting the impulse to scramble through her bag for a handkerchief until she'd gone a full block. It wouldn't do to get car grease on a cream-colored suit, she told herself as she wiped at the black smears her first Nowthen handshake had left on her fingers.

The property was easy to find, and, happily, it was everything one might expect from the home of a family carrying heavy insurance coverage.

The house itself—an elegant, pillared Colonial—waited graciously at the end of a long drive that meandered through a series of white-fenced paddocks. Frances caught a glimpse of low, well-kept stablelike buildings in the rear, and the air was heady with the fragrance of mock orange.

Very picturesque, she thought, if you liked that sort of thing.

No one answered the metallic thump of the front door knocker, so she walked around the house, her heels clicking importantly on the flagstone walk. The minute she rounded the back corner, she stopped and winced at her first glimpse of the building that had been destroyed by fire. Destruction of any sort was always ugly, she thought, but the ravages of fire were particularly unsettling. And particularly suspicious. Arson was the all-time favorite method of those who overinsured property, then destroyed it for the money.

The remnants of the building sat a good hundred yards from the house, and at first glance it was difficult to tell what function the building had served, there was so little left. A charred framework, a cement floor cluttered with burned timbers, bare, blackened studs that might have formed an interior wall—her best guess would have been that it was a multi-car garage, but from this distance the building seemed to have been empty.

Puzzled, she shielded her eyes from the noonday sun and frowned at the building, wishing the company president could have given her an idea of what kind of property had gone up in smoke. "You know as much as I do, Frances," he'd said. "The Harmons insure a lot of property with us; I have no idea what burned. We haven't been able to reach them since they first called their agent to report the fire. Phone lines could have burned, I suppose."

Frances sighed, staring at the ravaged building, then dropped her hand from her eyes and blew a stream of air up toward her forehead. It was hot for June, she realized suddenly, reaching to unbutton the jacket of her suit, wishing her legs weren't encased in nylon.

Suddenly a powerful-looking male figure dressed in jeans and a flapping denim shirt seemed to explode from a small white building off to the right. The metal bucket he carried clanged as he ran toward a bright red water pump jutting out of the ground halfway between them. Without so much as a glance in her direction, he grabbed the hose attached to the pump, turned the spigot, and directed a stream of water into the bucket.

"Hello!" Frances called out. "Mr. Harmon?"

From this distance all she could make out was a blond head jerking up, startled. She looked down distastefully at the bare earth between the flagstones she stood on and the distant pump, wondering what New Hampshire soil would do to two-hundred-dollar Italian heels. She decided not to find out. He'd come to her soon enough, then they'd go into the cool house, she'd introduce herself briefly, reassuring him that she was in town and on the job before checking into the hotel...

"Get the hell over here!" the man shouted, and she raised her head, her almond eyes rounding at the barked command. If the man had been close enough, he would have seen sunlight hit her eyes and burnish them gold. "Dammit, don't stand there gawking! Hurry up! I need you!''

Her eyes hardened and Frances prepared to turn and stalk away from such rudeness, but the pigtailed Frannie who still lived inside heard something in that hoarse shout that made her hesitate; a desperate quality she found herself responding to instinctively. Her narrow skirt made her run with mincing steps, and she grimaced every time a heel sank into the dirt.

"What?" she breathed anxiously when she finally reached him, but she barely had time to register a pair of crackling blue eyes in a strong, tanned face before he spun away to race back toward the little white building, water sloshing over the rim of the bucket as he ran.

"Hurry!" he called over his shoulder, and, spurred by the panic in his voice, Frances raced behind him as best she could. She stopped dead one step inside the building and scowled into the black interior, her nose wrinkling.

"Why, this is a *barn*."

"Of course it's a barn," he growled from somewhere just ahead and to her left. She squinted, trying to adjust her eyes to the dim light after the brightness of the noon sun. "What did you expect? Now get over here and hold this girl's head, or we're going to have another body to bury before sunset."

Frances caught her breath and froze. *Another* body?

"Come on!"

She followed his voice blindly, hands out-stretched before her, caught up in the man's desperation. Her shin banged into something metal and unyielding, but she barely felt it.

"Here." A large, rough hand grabbed hers, guided her to the right, then pulled her forward a few paces before pushing her to a stop. "I'll go in first. Wait here a minute."

Blinking, her eyes gradually adjusting to the gloom, she found herself in the doorway of a large stall cushioned with thick rubber mats. Gradually her vision focused on something in the center of the stall, and she repressed a shudder of revulsion.

A creature that looked like a cross between a storybook goat and an Afghan hound stood quivering on the wet black mats, eyes so wide that the whites showed all around the brown irises. One side of the little body boasted thick, shaggy, fawn-colored hair, but the other side was almost hairless, with blisters rising from angry pink skin. Frances thought she might faint. "Oh, dear," she murmured, overwhelmed by the horror of the animal's burns, and also by the overpowering smell of antiseptic in the enclosed space. "I'm really very sorry, but I don't think..."

Moving quickly, the blond man crossed the stall, knelt, then wrapped a gentle, restraining arm around the animal's neck and brought it down to lie on its hairy side. "Quick!" he hissed, breathing hard, dodging the frantic scrambling of four panicked legs while digging in the pocket of his shirt.

"Quick, *what*?"

"Dammit, get *over* here!"

It never occurred to her to question him, and later she would marvel at that, and then be irritated by it. For the moment, however, she forgot about her cream-colored suit and her expensive shoes and her revulsion, and moved quickly to kneel next to him simply because he had told her to. The rubber mats felt wet and sticky beneath her knees.

"Good," he grunted. "Now wrap your arm around her neck, right there..."

He had to be kidding. Wrap her arm around *that*? How could she even touch this wild, bleating thing with hair on one side and burns on the other, let alone restrain it...?

"...that's right...good. Just like that. Now lock your arm firmly, but gently...just try to keep her still..."

I am not doing this, Frances told herself, holding her breath, her eyes fastened on the far wall so she wouldn't have to look at what she was doing. In a very distant part of her mind she wondered if she was hurting this smelly, hairy, revolting thing; if it wouldn't be kinder to just let it go free. She caught a glimpse of a syringe in the man's hand and promptly closed her eyes.

"Hold on to her—that's it, just until I get the tranquilizer into her...there!"

Frances felt the convulsive tightening of the muscles in the neck beneath her arm, and then, after a moment, a loosening. She and the creature she held released simultaneous sighs. We're a duet, she thought giddily. Frances and the Amazing Sighing Thing.

"Okay, it's taking hold. I can get the IV started now. Put her head down gently."

She released the head with a shudder, and the man gave her a quick glance.

"Burns make you squeamish?"

"Apparently," she breathed, leaning back on her heels, bracing her hands on her thighs. She looked down at the mysterious creature, wincing at the blistered skin. She didn't know how long she looked at it, watching its breathing slow and then grow steady, its blinks become languid—but at some point she felt a surprising, almost painful tug at her heart. Whatever it was, it was just a baby, and no baby should have to suffer. "What is it, anyway?" she asked quietly.

The man was working a tube into a bottle that looked remarkably like any hospital's intravenous set-up. "It's a cow, of course. Or more precisely, a calf. What did you think she was?"

Frances looked again, then frowned sceptically. "That is *not* a cow!"

He chuckled quietly. "She's a Highlander— Scottish Highlander. They don't look much like the cows we're used to in this country, but she's a cow, nonetheless, and a valuable one at that.''

Frances cocked her head doubtfully. It didn't look *anything* like the cows she'd seen on television and in the movies and, occasionally, in fields that whizzed by her car at top speeds. Her brows tipped in compassion when it made a little noise that sounded more like a whimper than a moo. ''Is it still in pain?'' she asked.

''Not at the moment.''

Frances reached out tentatively to touch the creature's wide black nose, wondering if it would try to bite. She jerked her hand back when it nudged her fingers and made another sound. ''She was in the building that burned?''

He nodded absently, intent on taping the IV needle to the calf's leg.

''It was . . . a barn?''

He nodded again.

Frances sighed in disappointment and looked down at her lap. Barn fires were messy, time-consuming claims with virtually no promise of a bonus for uncovering fraud—farmers never burned down their own barns for the insurance money, especially not when there were animals inside.

She sighed again, discouraged, looking down at her stained skirt, feeling the wetness from the mats soak into her nylons, imagining all the men at Northeastern Casualty gathered in the boardroom, chuckling at the image of meticulous, unflappable Frances Hudson tiptoeing through manure piles in her city suits and shoes...

"She trusts you."

She jerked her head up, startled out of her miserable reverie.

The blond man was smiling at her. "The calf," he answered the question in her eyes. "She trusts you." He nodded down at the calf, and Frances was dumbfounded to see her own hand absently stroking the creature's neck. She pulled it quickly back to her lap and grabbed it with her other hand, as if to keep it from doing such a thing again.

"She shouldn't. I don't know the first thing about animals. I don't even like them."

"Well, that one likes you. And she ought to—you probably saved her life."

The words didn't sink in right away, but when they finally penetrated the wall of her discouragement she looked at the man with quiet surprise. "Saved her life?" she echoed softly.

He was crouched by the calf now, arms draped over his thighs, staring at her. He wasn't smiling...his features were perfectly still...and yet somehow she *felt* that he was, inside, where no one could see. "The burns would have healed, but the shock was killing her. If you hadn't been here to hold her so I could get the IV in..." His shrug completed the grim prognosis. "Thanks to you, she has a chance now."

Frances turned her head slowly to look down at the calf, and for a moment she didn't see the ghastly pink skin or the remains of tangled, matted hair—what she was was simply a small, helpless creature clinging desperately to life. That she might have played even a small part in the struggle filled her with wonder, and a strange sense of pride.

"You've ruined your clothes, I'm afraid."

She glanced down absently at a strand of fawn-colored hair on her stained skirt, then noticed clumps of the stuff stuck to the arm of her jacket. Funny, she should have been frantic about that. The suit was part of her image, after all, as were the expensive, now badly scuffed Italian shoes, and the silk stockings plastered wetly to her legs. Last week she'd fretted and worried for hours over a drop of coffee spilled on a silk blouse; today she was kneeling on a barn floor in a ruined suit, suspecting strongly that she didn't smell of Chanel No. 5 any more, and none of it seemed to matter very much.

She shrugged a little, oddly removed from it all, pushed herself to her feet, and pulled a stocking away from her knee. It snapped back with a sucking sound.

"That's just antiseptic solution. I washed the mats down with it earlier. It isn't the worst thing you could kneel in in a barn, you know."

Frances surprised herself by smiling at that. "No, I suppose it isn't."

He was looking up at her now, arms still draped over his thighs, his head tipped to one side, his expression stern. His blue eyes were quietly intent, two spots of color in a face streaked with dust and badly in need of a shave. It was a powerful face, Frances thought, appraising it as she automatically appraised everything. One of those strongly drawn male faces you saw on museum statuary and nowhere else.

"You ever need a job, let me know. I can always use someone who has a way with animals."

The offer made her smile, partly because it flattered her in a strange way, but mostly because she hadn't spent the last six years scrambling up the business ladder to end up as a farm worker. "Thanks anyway, but I already have a job, Mr. Harmon."

A broad smile slashed the tan of his face, transforming it from museum statuary to flesh and blood, and, through some trick of the light, it seemed to brighten the whole barn. Seeing those carved features come to life with a smile was like watching fireworks spangle the black of a night sky. "I take it you haven't met Franklin Harmon," he observed.

Frances hesitated. "You're not...?"

"Not even close. I'm Ethan Alexander, Franklin's vet. And you?"

"Frances," she murmured, unaware that her features had softened. "Frances Hudson," she added, transfixed by his eyes. She'd seen that particular shade of blue somewhere before; she just couldn't remember where.

"Hello, Frances." He was rising to his feet now, offering his hand, and she had to lift her chin to keep his face in view. He was very tall, very broad in the shoulder.

Her second Nowthen handshake was warm and dry and rough, and it would leave her palm smelling faintly of calf and her knees a little wobbly.

After too long a moment, she remembered to pull her hand from his. "I'm here to investigate Mr. Harmon's claim."

"His claim?" His voice was rich and deep and melodious...why hadn't she noticed that right away? The sound of it made her feel giddy, almost weightless.

She blinked, licked her lips, tried to find that firm centre of composure that had somehow slipped away. "His insurance claim for the fire. I'm from the Northeastern Casualty office in Boston."

"Oh-h." He nodded slowly and his expression seemed to flatten a little. "They sent an investigator all the way from Boston?"

Something in his voice made her wary. "Of course."

"Good Lord," he mumbled, more to himself than to her. "You'd think they'd have the sense to send someone local..." He let the sentence fade away with an exasperated shake of his head, and Frances stiffened defensively, feeling like an unwelcome intruder.

"We don't happen to have any investigators living in Nowthen."

"You're from the city," he said flatly, and somehow the statement sounded like a condemnation.

"You have something against people from the city?"

He barked an unpleasant laugh. "I have a lot against people from the city, but that's not the point. The point is, a city investigator doesn't know the first thing about barn fires and has no business pretending he does." Saying the word "he" made him pause and look at her. "It's even worse that you're a woman."

Frances could feel her eyes narrowing to yellow flashes of light, her blood-pressure rising to flood her face with colour. "Well," she said, her voice frigid, "I don't suppose you can get much more worthless than that. A woman, and a woman from the city to boot. I'm surprised I wasn't shot on sight!"

His lips worked in a frantic effort to suppress a smile, and that made Frances angrier then ever. She didn't know which was worse—being blatantly insulted, or being laughed at for taking offense. Because she wasn't sure what else to do, she turned on her heel and started to walk away.

"I only meant that woman are gentler creatures than men," he said from behind her. "And that's the way it's supposed to be. But gentle creatures shouldn't have to deal with the aftermath of a barn fire."

"'Gentle creatures,' indeed!" Frances bit down on an angry retort and stomped away, furious to be so openly patronized.

"You ever investigate a barn fire before?" he called after her.

"I investigate fires all the time," she snapped over her shoulder.

"*Barn* fires?"

She kept on walking.

"Hey!"

She turned in the barn's narrow passageway and glared back at where he stood next to the calf's stall. He should have looked smaller from this distance, but for some reason he didn't. He seemed to fill the passage.

"Where are you going?" he demanded.

She scowled hard, hoping he could see in the dim light the terrible look on her face. "None of your business."

His low chuckle echoed the length of the alleyway, making her response sound childish. "Everything that happens in Nowthen is everybody's business."

"What an excellent argument for living anywhere else!" she retorted.

Something about the quality of the silence that followed made her relieved when he broke it. "The Harmons aren't home, if you were thinking about heading up to the house. Won't be, until nightfall. You'll have to come back then."

She shifted her shoulders under her jacket, turned, and began to walk away again.

"I'll see you later, Frances Hudson."

She faltered once, then continued to walk. "I certainly hope not," she said without turning around.

Her lips clamped together in mild frustration as she continued to walk back out into the noonday sun, head high, wondering if his eyes were really burning into her back or if it only felt that way.

Suddenly she felt a very long, long way from Boston.

CHAPTER TWO

FRANCES made the trip from Harmon's farm back into Nowthen in record time, partly because she found her own company in the car almost unbearably offensive. Even with the windows wide open she could still smell the cloying odors of barn and antiseptic clinging to her clothes, her hair, her hands. She wrinkled her nose, wondering why anyone would choose to be a vet if it meant you had to smell like this all the time.

I'll bet he's not married, she thought with vicious satisfaction. I'll bet he can't even get a date, smelling like that, no matter how good-looking he is...

She slammed the brakes on her thoughts, irritated that she was still thinking of Ethan Alexander at all, and concentrated on the scenery.

Even in a farming valley like this one, New Hampshire's White Mountains hovered in the background like menacing guardians, blocking the view. Frances missed the uninterrupted view of Boston facing the endless expanse of ocean; the sense that there was always somewhere else to go.

These cloistered mountain valleys made her almost claustrophobic, pretty as they were with their patchwork fields of new crops, their clusters of wildflowers crowding the road. She sped past a particularly riotous patch of blooms on her left, thinking they were almost the same peacock-blue color as the country vet's eyes . . .

Peacock. That was the color of his eyes—just like the iridescent circles on the male peacock's tail at the Boston zoo. She sniffed haughtily, thinking it was a stupid color for a man's eyes to be; an unnatural color; and then she drove into Nowthen scowling, because here she was, thinking about him again.

The only hotel in town was a converted turn-of-the-century house on the western arc of the village green. As Frances stood at the blocky registration desk in the old-fashioned lobby, signing her name in a dusty, leather-bound book, she wondered if all the people who lived in this town were as backward as the accommodation. There was no bellboy, no elevator, and no room service. "This isn't the city, you know," the taciturn woman at the desk pointed out.

No kidding, Frances thought as she lugged her own bags up the broad staircase to her second-floor room. The minute the door closed behind her she stripped off her clothes, bagged the lot in plastic, and hurried to shower away the pervasive odors of barn and antiseptic that reminded her of a morning she wanted to forget.

Her stomach was growling by the time she finished towel drying her hair, but she took her time unpacking, then dressed as carefully as she would have for lunch at one of Boston's finest restaurants. When she was satisfied that her image was once again intact—white Oxford shirt, navy trousers and jacket, bright caramel hair pulled back into its customary coil—she went downstairs for lunch.

The hotel's dining room was surprisingly large, considering that there was only one other customer...a man, sitting at one of the window tables across the room, gazing out at the village green. He turned his head when she entered, then stood abruptly.

"Hello again, Miss Hudson." The backlight from the window kept his features in shadow, but she'd already learned to recognize that voice in the dark.

"Hello, Mr. Alexander," she said with a cool nod. She took a table far from his in the middle of the room, sat with her back toward him, and snapped her napkin open on her lap. Almost before she had registered the sound of his steps crossing the room, he was pulling out the chair opposite her and sitting down.

"Silly to make Margaret wait on two tables since we're the only customers, don't you think?" His hair was damp from a recent shower, spiking in blond peaks on the top of his head. He wore a clean white shirt open at the throat, with sleeves rolled up to expose tanned, muscular forearms. Frances wished she hadn't noticed that. She made up for it by speaking a little more sharply than she had intended.

"Shouldn't you still be out at the Harmons' taking care of that calf?"

"For a woman who claims she doesn't like animals, you seem awfully concerned about that calf," he said with a grin.

Frances made a face and turned away.

"But you don't have to worry, my assistant is with her. I'll get a call if I'm needed." He looked her up and down briefly and frowned. "Don't you own anything but suits? You can't go poking through a charred building in that outfit."

She gave him a withering look. "My overalls are at the cleaners."

He tried unsuccessfully to suppress a smile, leaning back in his chair until it balanced on two legs.

"Besides, I have no intention of 'poking through a charred building.' The arson squad will do that."

His chair came down with an abrupt thump and he stared up at her, dumbfounded. "The arson squad? What are you talking about?"

She hesitated for a moment, surprised by his reaction. "The arson squad," she repeated carefully. "They'll examine the fire site for evidence of arson, then file their report with me."

He was perfectly still, and perfectly quiet, but he hadn't taken his eyes off her. When he finally spoke, it was so softly that Frances could barely hear him. "I certainly hope you're not suggesting that Franklin burned down his own barn."

Frances hesitated, startled by the sudden menace in his tone. "I... I'm not suggesting anything. Statistically, barn fires are almost always accidental. It's just that an arson investigation is standard in fire claims. Company policy."

He continued to stare into her eyes for a moment, as if he could read what was behind them, then nodded once. "All right, I guess that makes sense, from an insurance company's point of view. Still, I wouldn't use the word arson in the same sentence with Franklin's name if I were you. Not in this town."

Frances twitched a little at the veiled threat.

"And if you want any investigating done, you'll have to do it yourself. Nowthen doesn't have an arson squad. We have a five-man volunteer fire department, and they don't write reports."

Frances pressed her lips together and frowned. She wasn't *that* kind of an investigator. She didn't sift through fire damage in white overalls and a surgical mask, collecting evidence in little plastic bags. She barely knew what to look for. Her job was to follow behind the people who did the dirty work, to collate and evaluate what they had found. It was a nice, clean, safe job that she usually performed in a nice, clean, safe office.

Then again, she thought ruefully, why should this stupid assignment start to get easier now? She released a long sigh of frustration and looked around impatiently. "Aren't there any waitresses in this place?"

"Margaret!" his voice boomed instantly, making her jump. Almost immediately a broad, rosy face crowned with a frizz of salt-and-pepper hair poked through a swinging door on the far side of the room. Frances recognized her as the woman behind the registration desk. "Save yourself a trip, Margaret, and bring us a couple of specials. I'll draw the beers." The woman made a circle with her thumb and forefinger and disappeared. "There's no lunch menu to speak of," Ethan explained, "but I can vouch for anything Margaret puts on a plate. Sit tight; I'll get the beer."

"She's the cook too?" Frances asked.

"The cook, the desk clerk, the waitress... and the owner of this place. We don't specialize much in a town this size."

Frances sat in numbed silence when he left the table. She was farther from Boston than she'd thought, in a town without an arson squad, in a restaurant without menus, about to swill beer in her good clothes with a man who probably thought women were at their best barefoot and pregnant. She wondered if he'd bring a glass, or if she'd have to drink out of a can.

When he returned he was carrying two heavy glass mugs foaming white at the top, frosty gold beneath. "A hot day needs a cold beer." He took his seat and raised his mug in a perfunctory toast. He drained a full third of the glass before setting it down and looking at her. He had very long eyelashes. They made spiky shadows on his cheekbones when he blinked. "Aren't you thirsty?"

Frances glanced quickly down at her glass, took a single, cautious sip, then followed it with another. It was surprisingly good, and the cold taste, the tickle of the foam on her upper lip, brought back an instant flood of childhood memories. Block parties in the stifling evenings of midsummer, the drab streets brightened with banners and laughter and music, and Uncle Arthur giving her her first taste of beer when she was only ten...

"You're not drinking. Would you rather have something else?"

She snapped back to the present with a hard blink and wondered how long she'd been staring off into the distance of the past. "No, this is fine. It's just that I haven't had a beer in years..." She lost the rest of her sentence when she looked at Ethan Alexander.

He was leaning forward, his forearms braced on the table. The blue of his eyes seemed lighter, like the color of a winter lake before the ice thickened into white. Frances met his stare boldly for a moment, then something she saw behind his eyes made her want to drop her gaze. Concentrating fiercely, she managed to keep her eyes focused on his for another full five seconds before she felt the color rushing to her face, and had to look away. Happily the woman called Margaret chose that moment to bustle through the door, an enormous tray of food braced on one plump shoulder. "I'll bring coffee when you're finished," she said, leaving as quickly as she'd come.

Frances and Ethan ate in relative silence, stealing glances at one another that were much more profound, much more revealing than anything they might have said. Distracted, Frances started with little appetite, but after the first few bites the food became the distraction, overshadowing the crackling tension between them.

"You like Margaret's cooking," he understated, watching her fill her plate from the serving dishes for a second time.

She stopped at that and stared at the huge mounds of food on her plate, as if someone else had put them there when she wasn't looking. "You don't get food like this in Boston restaurants," she explained, a little embarrassed. "It's like a picnic; just like . . ." Her eyes roamed over the dishes of baked beans, potato salad, thick slabs of cold meat and freshly baked bread.

"Like what?" he prompted.

"Like the cold suppers Mom used to lay out for company." She toyed with her fork, looking down, remembering. He was watching her intently, but Frances didn't notice.

When Margaret came in to clear the table, Frances smiled up at her. "That was a fabulous meal. Thank you." It worried her that the older woman bustled away hurriedly, obviously flustered. "Did I say something wrong?"

Ethan almost smiled. "Not wrong—just unexpected. People like you don't usually appreciate Margaret's down-home cooking."

Frances eyed him suspiciously. "People like me?"

"City people," he explained.

Her mouth twitched as she tried to decide just how angry to be. She finally settled on something halfway between out-and-out rage and chilly indignation. "You don't think much of anyone who isn't from Nowthen, do you?"

His smile was mischievous. "What gives you that idea?"

She spoke slowly, carefully, enunciating each word. "First you didn't think I could investigate a local fire claim; now you're telling me I can't even appreciate good food. You make it sound like all people from the city are alien life forms..."

"You are, in a way." Ethan shrugged amiably. "Boston's a long way from Nowthen. Values are different here."

Exasperated, Frances let her fork clatter to her plate. She could almost feel the spark of yellow flaring in her eyes. "That's the most prejudiced remark I've ever heard! You think your values are better than mine, just because you happen to live out in the middle of nowhere?"

His smile broadened with amusement. "You said 'better,' I didn't. I said 'different.'"

"So what's different?" she snapped.

"Look around." He spread his palm in affected innocence. "People in this town don't take much notice of designer clothes, pretentious cars——"

"My car is *not* pretentious," she said carefully, trying to control her temper. "It's reliable transportation..."

"That car isn't *transportation*." He made a mockery of the word. "It's a statement, telling everyone who sees it that you can afford it, that you're a success. You don't buy a car like that to get you from one point to another; you buy a car like that to impress people."

Frances straightened in her chair, bristling visibly, just barely managing to hold her tongue. She wanted to fire back an angry retort, but what he'd said was just too close to the truth. Finally she took a deep breath and blew it out through her cheeks. "In some careers, maintaining a certain image is important," she said shortly.

"Then maybe you've chosen the wrong career."

She forced a saccharine smile. "I suppose you think I'd do better as a vet's assistant. That was your suggestion this morning, wasn't it?"

His grin widened. "Not exactly, but yes, now that you mention it, I think you'd do very well as my assistant."

Frances rolled her eyes. "Well, you couldn't be more wrong. As I told you, I've never liked animals, and they've never liked me..."

"The calf did."

Her brows twitched in confusion.

"And you liked the calf." He looked right at her, and there was no mockery in his smile now. "Admit it—you're still worried about her. I can see it in your eyes."

She dropped her gaze and frowned, remembering in vivid detail the image of that pathetic, burned creature looking up at her with a trusting expression that was almost human. "I'm just not used to seeing anything suffer like that, that's all," she mumbled. "I don't know how you stand it, seeing animals in pain all the time. What on earth possesses someone to be a vet?"

"Wanting to stop the pain," he replied simply, eyeing her thoughtfully over the rim of his cup. "I'll take you out to see the fire damage now, if you like. I don't think you should wait much longer."

"Why not?"

"Because it's hot."

"Then doesn't it make more sense to wait until it cools off?"

Ethan frowned hard at her, as if she was being particularly thick-headed. "Bodies ripen in heat, you know."

Frances blanched and her eyes flew wide. "Bodies?" she said weakly, regretting every bite of the lunch she'd just eaten.

"The cattle Franklin lost in the fire," he explained, a puzzled frown tipping his brows. "The bull, especially. He was a big loss. Insured for a quarter of a million, I think, maybe more."

"Cattle," Frances intoned dully. "The insured property was...a cow?"

"Seven cows, actually, and one bull."

"I see." She took a deep breath and cleared her throat.

"We moved them out to the back pasture this morning, but if you want a look at them it'll have to be now. They'll be buried by nightfall...would you like a drink of water or something?"

She shook her head mutely.

"What did you think the Harmons lost in that fire, Miss Hudson?"

"Oh, I don't know...antiques, artwork, something like that..." She shrugged, and let the sentence trail away.

He released a long, exasperated sigh. "I told you this was no job for someone from the city. Have you ever seen an animal that's been burned to death?"

"Dear God, no!" she whispered, so horrified at the prospect that she didn't notice he'd slandered city people once again.

He sighed and looked across the room. "It isn't going to be pleasant, you know."

Frances forced what she hoped was a superior smile. "There are a lot of things in the city that aren't pleasant too, Mr. Alexander. I'm not totally naive."

Ethan eyed her steadily for a moment. "You sure you can handle this?"

"Of course I'm sure," she said crisply. "I'll be fine, just fine."

But she wasn't fine, unless being fine meant fainting dead away in the arms of a virtual stranger. Even in the open space of Franklin Harmon's back pasture, even with the unrecognizable carcasses of the cattle still a full twenty feet away, Frances had taken one look at the row of bald, pink and black blistered bodies, another at the bulldozer in front of them, blade lowered menacingly, and the world had gone black. Next thing she knew she was propped in the front seat of the pickup truck that had brought them here and Ethan Alexander was holding a Thermos lid of cool water to her lips.

"Here, take another sip. Feel better?"

She shook her head weakly.

"I told you it wouldn't be pleasant. Just sit there for a minute, catch your breath. The wooziness will pass."

Frances closed her eyes and tried to ignore the clammy feel of perspiration drying on her forehead, the unnatural pitch and roll of her stomach. Ethan Alexander sat quietly behind the wheel, looking straight ahead, giving her the time she needed. A full five minutes passed before she felt she could talk without risk of fainting all over again. "I've never seen anything like that in my life," she mumbled.

"Most people haven't."

"I've never fainted in my life, either."

"There's no shame in fainting."

Frances smiled weakly. "There is where I come from."

He turned to face her, cocking his right leg up on the seat between them. "People don't faint in Boston?"

She let her head fall back on the seat and closed her eyes. "I don't like animals," she mumbled, as if she were reminding herself of the fact. "This shouldn't have bothered me."

He sighed heavily and looked past her out of the side window. "Maybe you weren't seeing dead animals. Maybe you were just seeing death." His eyes shifted to meet hers, and she saw a depth behind them she hadn't noticed before. "Like I don't really see animals when I'm trying to save them. I just see life."

She rolled her head to look at him, a little surprised to hear philosophy from a country vet. "You're a strange man," she murmured, silently noting the clean, pure beauty of his face when he turned it toward her. "I'm surprised you aren't a doctor, feeling the way you do."

"I am a doctor," he told her.

"I mean a people doctor."

He looked away and shrugged, and Frances had the feeling he was staring at something far beyond the field outside the windshield. "Why don't you like animals?" he asked.

"Because you can't trust them. You never know what they're thinking or when they'll turn on you."

His laugh sounded harsh. "And people are so different?"

She blinked at him thoughtfully, sensing a window opening on to the depth she'd seen in his eyes just a moment before. "Most of them are," she answered quietly, thinking of her mother, her uncle, the kindness of all the people that sometimes pushed the bitter memories of poverty aside.

"You're the product of a charmed life," he said caustically, and Frances couldn't help herself; she laughed out loud.

Ethan jerked his head and frowned at her curiously, and she stiffened and turned away. She hadn't meant to reveal so much.

"I'm feeling much better now," she said firmly. "Could you take me back to the hotel, please?"

He stared at her for a moment, then nodded silently, started the truck, and guided it over the gash the bulldozer had made in the field, back toward the highway.

CHAPTER THREE

FRANCES awoke the next morning to a gray, sodden sky that glowered outside her hotel room window. For the first time in her memory, she was tempted to pull the covers over her head and go back to sleep. She felt none of her customary enthusiasm to be up and about the challenges of a new day, and only force of habit finally sent her rolling reluctantly from the room's cozy four-poster bed.

The mirror showed shadows lying under her eyes that even makeup couldn't hide completely—mute testimony to a sleep troubled by nightmares she couldn't remember—and this subtle alteration of her appearance worried her much more than the sleep she had lost. Losing control of the image Frances Katharine Hudson presented to the world was the first step of losing Frances Katharine Hudson altogether.

She dressed hurriedly in a plain black suit that reflected her mood, but she had trouble with her hair. Wayward strands of caramel kept snaking out of the coil to dangle crazily down her back. And there was something wrong with her eyes this morning too. They seemed darker than normal, more brown than amber, and that changed the entire aspect of her face, making it seem that her features had somehow softened during the night.

She applied her makeup with even more care than usual, but it didn't help. The image in the mirror wasn't the pigtailed Frannie she was always afraid of seeing; but she wasn't the cool, sophisticated woman who had looked back at her yesterday morning either. She didn't know who she was. Finally she turned from the mirror in disgust and left the hotel to drive out to the Harmon farm.

A sense of command, of being in control, revived briefly once she was behind the wheel of her car. By the second mile on the rain-slicked two-lane road she had regained a fair measure of composure, but as the third mile slid beneath the wet slap of her tires on the road, she had begun to remember her behavior yesterday. Most of it had been totally out of character. First there had been the baffling sense of affinity with the injured calf; then that childish, purely physical attraction to Ethan Alexander; and last, but certainly not least, that pathetic, contemptible fainting spell. That alone had left her so undone that she hadn't even waited for the Harmons to return home.

"I'll meet with them tomorrow," she'd told Ethan unsteadily on the way back to the hotel, and that had been the sum of their conversation. She had fled the truck almost before he'd come to a complete stop, and her face burned with embarrassment even now to remember that rapid, almost panicked exit. He had told her that this was no job for a woman, and she had told him that she could do her job as well as any man... and then she had lost control not only of her image, but of her body as well, fainting like some simpering Southern belle with the vapors, proving him right in the most eloquent fashion. The most she could hope for was that she would never encounter Ethan Alexander again; that she would never have to face those strange blue eyes that had seen a chink in her armor even before she'd known it was there.

The clouds had renewed their steady, morose drizzle by the time she drove around to the back of the Harmon house. Through the steady slapping of the wiper blades, she saw Ethan running from the barn to the house, a windbreaker held over his head, and swore softly. She was to be spared nothing, then. He veered toward the car when he saw her, stopped to jerk her door open, and greeted her with a grin.

"Come on, I'm getting soaked. We've been waiting for you."

Frances forced a weak smile, searched his eyes for a hint of contempt, but saw none. "I didn't know you'd be here," she said lamely.

"Of course I'm here. I knew you were coming." He grabbed her hand and pulled her gently from the car out into the drizzle, and she

wanted to tell him to stop that, to let her go for
a minute, to leave her in privacy so she could
mull over what he'd just said—but his hand was
insistent, and instead she found herself trotting
quickly up the walk toward the back door, her
hand locked firmly in his.

Elaine Harmon opened the door and hustled
them in with a flutter of hands and a chorus of
tongue-cluckings at Ethan's dripping hair. She
was an unpretentious, motherly figure with a cap
of fluffy gray hair, a floral-print house dress
spread over a large frame, and an obvious affection for Ethan Alexander. Her clothes and her
manner seemed strangely incongruous with the
streamlined, hi-tech kitchen they entered, and
Frances couldn't help thinking that she looked
like a farm wife caught by mistake in the house
of a society matron.

"Oh, Ethan!" She wrapped plump, sun-
burned arms around his neck and her eyes filled
with tears. "Beth just left. She said she didn't
know if the calf would make it."

Ethan held her gently, then eased her away just
far enough to smile down at her. "We'll do our
best, Elaine. She's got a lot of fight in her yet.
Did Tommy come to relieve Beth?"

She nodded and sighed. "He's out there now,
with his sleeping bag and that awful cassette deck
of his. You sure he knows what to do?"

"He's every bit as competent as Beth, Elaine. He'll be a full-fledged vet himself this time next year."

"I know, I know. But Beth has always been so good with animals, even if she didn't have the schooling. Tommy's so...clinical."

"Beth is my full-time assistant," Ethan explained in an aside to Frances. "She was born and raised in Nowthen, which makes her eminently trustworthy; Tommy, on the other hand, is a summer intern from out of town, and therefore immediately suspect."

Like me, Frances thought.

"This is Frances Hudson, Elaine, the investigator from Northeastern Casualty I told you about." He stepped to one side and Frances felt her hand enveloped by yet another Nowthen handshake. "She has a few questions for you, if you have time."

Mrs. Harmon focused kind brown eyes on Frances and smiled. "Oh, my! You're perfectly lovely, aren't you, child?"

The professional greeting Frances had prepared stuttered to a halt in her mind. Suddenly she didn't feel like a cool, self-assured professional meeting a client. She felt like a little girl meeting someone's mother for the first time. "Er—thank you. I'm pleased to meet you, Mrs. Harmon."

"Oh, poof to the Mrs. Harmon nonsense! Call me Elaine. Now come along and sit down, you two. I have coffee and rolls waiting, and all those dreadful policy papers scattered all over the kitchen table. Can't imagine how you make sense of all that legal mumbo jumbo, Frannie.''

Her mother called her Frannie. No one else, because no one else had known the pigtailed child who had gone by that name. Hearing it from a stranger's lips was oddly disturbing, and oddly comforting, all at the same time.

Frances took a seat opposite Ethan at a large chrome and glass table and reluctantly accepted a cinnamon roll and a mug of coffee. She listened to Ethan and Elaine converse with the easy familiarity of two people who cared very much for one another, and then asked as few questions as she possibly could. For all her superficial good cheer, there were dark shadows under Mrs. Harmon's eyes and a visible tension behind the smile. Clearly the trauma of the fire had taken its toll, and Frances felt profoundly guilty for asking her to recall it.

She learned that the fire had started some time after midnight; that Mr. and Mrs. Harmon had been wakened by the frantic bawling of the cattle, but not in time to save them. ''Franklin tried, of course—would have burned himself to a crisp if I hadn't been there to hold him back—but it just went too fast. The building was almost gone by the time the fire department and ambulance got here.''

''Ambulance?'' queried Frances.

Elaine nodded miserably. "Crazy old man burned both his hands—second degree, thank heaven so he won't lose the use of them, but he'll be in the hospital for another day or two."

Frances felt her face stiffen with disbelief at the thought of a man risking his life just to save an animal's. Half a million dollars or not, the last suspicion that the fire might have been set intentionally vanished. "I'm sorry," she murmured. "I didn't know Mr. Harmon was hurt. Any idea how the fire started?"

"None. And no idea why the smoke alarms didn't work, either. We had a battery of them installed and wired to the house when we put up that building, but we never heard an alarm." Elaine pressed a hand briefly to her eyes, then looked up, her eyes moist. "You'll have to excuse me. We both loved that damn bull, and the cows too, for that matter. I know it sounds silly, but you can get real attached to animals you care for after a while."

Frances felt a tug of real sympathy, not for the animals that had died, but for the woman who obviously felt the loss. "I think that's all I need for now," she said. "I have some background work that will keep me pretty busy for the next few days, but I'll start processing the claim just as soon as I can."

Mrs. Harmon smiled at her.

"I think I'll go examine the fire site now while you two talk, if you don't mind."

Mrs. Harmon gave her a motherly frown. "Mind that pretty suit of yours, Frannie. Didn't you bring any old clothes?"

Frances coloured slightly at the sight of Ethan barely suppressing a smile. "Thank you, but I'll be careful."

She'd just started to circle the outside of the burned barn when she heard a faint mewling from the small building off to the right. She cocked her head to listen more carefully. The sound came again, more insistent this time, drawing her helplessly to its source.

She found the calf alone, its IV line tangled around one leg, big brown eyes rolling back to look at her plaintively. Frances hesitated at the stall entrance, her lower lip caught between her teeth. "Where's Tommy?" she asked the calf, and had to chastize herself for actually waiting for a reply. "Oh, boy, I'm really losing it," she grumbled, stepping into the stall. "Twenty-four hours in this stupid town and already I'm not only talking to animals; I'm waiting for them to answer!"

The calf bleated at that, and Frances pressed her lips into an angry line to keep from smiling.

Her eyes followed the tangled IV line to where the tension had partially dislodged the needle. She shuddered, wondering if she dared try to fix it herself, or if she should just get Ethan. The calf made the decision for her by struggling to free its leg, dislodging the needle even further.

Without another conscious thought, Frances dropped to her knees, draping one arm around the calf's neck to quiet it, untangling the IV line with her other hand. With the tension off the line, the needle automatically slid back into its proper place, and the calf sighed.

"Poor baby," murmured Frances as the broad black nose burrowed into her side. "Where is that damn Tommy, anyway? How could he leave you alone like this? There, there, it's all right now..." She continued a mindless, soothing crooning as she stroked the calf's neck, unaware of the tall figure that had moved silently into the stall doorway.

"Frannie."

Her eyes flew wide and she froze at the sound of Ethan's voice, suddenly realizing what a picture she must make, the woman who hated animals kneeling once again in a barn stall.

Before she could engineer the move to her feet, Ethan was crouched beside her, looking at her with tender amusement. "You've ruined another suit," he said with a quiet smile. "You're just like a kid, you know? Always getting your clothes dirty." He plucked at the sleeve of her jacket. "You don't belong in this kind of an outfit anyway. You belong in blue jeans and tennis shoes, with your hair down." Before she could register what he was doing, he had reached behind her head to pull free the pins which held the coil of her hair. The back of her neck tingled as he ran his fingers through the compressed strands to liberate them, and her lips parted in surprise.

"There," he said, smiling, "that's better. Now you look more like yourself. Now we're getting a look at the *real* Frannie."

Frances just stared at him for a moment, stunned, then jumped to her feet, away from his hand, panic-stricken. He was seeing the girl she always expected to see in the mirror; little pig-tailed Frannie in the hand-me-down dresses. "You're wrong," she whispered frantically. "This *is* the real Frances."

She gestured desperately at her suit, her shoes, and then her hair. But her suit was soiled, her shoes were scuffed, her hair was flowing over her shoulders, and she realized she was proving his point more than hers.

"Frannie, Frannie," he murmured, rising to his feet to look down at her, his hand reaching out to cup her chin, "what are you so afraid of?"

She couldn't remember. Not with the heat of his fingers under her chin, the piercing fire in those remarkable blue eyes. The eyes hypnotized her, robbed her of the power to move, to think; even if his hand hadn't shifted to encircle her neck, to hold her captive, she would have been as helpless to move.

She was vaguely aware of the warmth of his breath as his face bent towards hers, and then the searing brush of his lips against her mouth. Her breath caught in her throat, then was expelled in a rush as his arms swept her against his chest. The physical sensations raging through her body were totally unfamiliar. What was this mysterious heat, rising from the pit of her stomach to threaten the edge of her reason, like molten lava trembling on the lip of a sleeping volcano? What was this sudden numbness in her limbs which all but paralyzed her?

Suddenly his hands were cradling her face, one thumb tentatively stroking the swollen bud of her lower lip. "Frannie," he whispered hoarsely, and than again, "Frannie."

The force of his mouth against hers, the almost cruel pressure of her breasts flattening against his chest, left her breathless at first, then shocked her into a sudden awareness of what she was allowing to happen. What *Frannie* was allowing to happen.

"No!" She pushed herself violently from him, taking a few quick, unsteady steps backward, her eyes wide and wary.

He didn't move, and somehow Frances found that more ominous than if he had tried to overpower her. He just stood there, bright strands of blond quivering over his brow. His rain-soaked T-shirt clung to his chest, outlining the musculature that rose and fell rapidly with his breath. Bright slices of blue burned through the shuttered lids of his eyes.

"Excuse me," Frances breathed in panicked, automatic politeness that was silly under the circumstances. She moved quickly to push past him, only to find herself spun violently around when his hand snaked out to grasp her wrist.

"You're running away from yourself, Frannie, not me." His voice was as gentle as his grip on her wrist was harsh. "You're running from the woman who cares about a wounded calf; you're running from the woman who fainted when she saw death...and, maybe most of all, you're running from the woman who felt desire for a man. That's the worst, isn't it, Frannie? Coming face-to-face with what you really are—a woman."

"Stop calling me Frannie!" she tried to shout, but it sounded more like a whimper.

"'Stop calling me Frannie,'" he repeated tonelessly, the light in his eyes fading. "That's it in a nutshell, isn't it? Frannie is the woman you're afraid to be; the woman you're running from." He released her wrist abruptly, and held her only with his eyes. "But you're not running fast enough, Frannie," he whispered.

She'd been trying to break and run from him for so long that she was totally dumbfounded when he was the one to turn and walk away without another word, without a single backward glance, leaving her alone. She jumped a little when the calf bleated softly behind her.

Well, maybe not totally alone.

CHAPTER FOUR

FRANCES snatched the last suit jacket from its padded hanger, raced to the bed, jammed it into the already bulging suitcase, and slammed down the lid. Pieces of silk and linen protruded from the closed case like accusing fabric fingers, but Frances didn't notice. She worked rapidly, mindlessly, driven by the unconscious need to escape. Her mind had not yet articulated what she was escaping from or where she was escaping to; she knew only that everything she had learned to value was somehow threatened by every additional minute she spent in Nowthen.

She hurried into the bathroom to shove a case full of cosmetics into the gaping mouth of her overnight bag, but froze when she caught sight of her panicked reflection. Roses of pink blossomed high on her cheeks, contrasting sharply with the otherwise pallid landscape of her face. Rain-dampened waves clung wetly to her neck and trailed dark lines of moisture over the black jacket of her suit.

Heavens, she thought, sinking to the edge of the bath, facing the mirror, frightened by her own reflection. Who is that?

Nothing in this world could have terrified Frances half as much as losing what she had worked so many years to gain. Her image was the physical evidence of that achievement that she carried with her everywhere. Now, abruptly, it was gone. It was as if the past eight years— the years she had struggled to climb from inner city poverty to the towers of downtown Boston— had been erased.

It's nothing, she tried to reassure herself. A shower, a little makeup, the proper clothes— that's all it will take to bring it all back—but, even in the privacy of her own mind, her thoughts sounded frantic. Somehow this assignment was robbing her of the essence of Frances Katharine Hudson—the part of her that thought the meaning of life could be found in season tickets for the Philharmonic, first edition prints, and a designer wardrobe. The things were all still there, but the magic of possessing them was gone. How could such a thing have happened in the small space of a day?

And that, of course, was what she was running from. Not from Nowthen or the wounded calf or even Ethan Alexander, but from what all these things were showing her about herself.

She dropped her head into her hands and felt the tickle of her loosened hair cascading over her fingers. She was suddenly, overwhelmingly weary, like a long-distance runner who had finally sur- rendered to the body's cry for rest.

In the back of her mind, she had formulated a vague plan to hurry back to Boston, to the home that was the treasure house of her possessions, thinking that somehow she would be safe there. But in the bleak, fluorescent light of a small-town hotel bathroom, she came to the even bleaker realization that there *was* no safe harbor, no place to hide from this strange, unfamiliar woman in the mirror—except the one place everyone could find escape from anything—in sleep.

She walked woodenly to the bed, pushed the suitcase to one side, and curled up next to it like a dazed, overtired baby finally settling down for a nap. The digital bedside clock read 11:30 a.m., and her last conscious thought was that she'd never be able to fall asleep in the middle of the day. In the next instant her eyelids fluttered, then closed. While she slept, the rain stopped, the clouds broke, and the clock ate away the afternoon.

The phone jarred her awake, shooting her heart with the kind of adrenalin jolt that would have prepared her ancestors for flight from danger. Confused, half asleep, she groped for the receiver and mumbled "hello" into the mouthpiece.

"Frannie? Is that you?"

She was instantly, fully awake. She'd phoned her mother last night to give her the hotel number, never imagining that she would ever use it. Unless...

"My God, what is it? What's wrong?"

There was a brief pause on the other end of the line, then a cautious, puzzled voice. "Why, nothing's wrong, nothing at all. I'm downstairs in the lobby, and I thought I might be able to talk you into joining me for supper. Did I catch you at a bad time?"

Frances felt the abrupt loosening of all the muscles she had unconsciously tensed, and she released a quiet sigh of relief. It wasn't her mother; it was Elaine Harmon.

"Supper?" she asked, confused because she hadn't even eaten lunch yet. Her eyes widened when she caught sight of the clock. The 4:30 p.m. read-out seemed like an accusation of all the time she'd lost.

"Actually, it's more like an old-time social than supper," Elaine was saying. "There's a concert in the bandstand in the park, food booths, that sort of thing. We do it once a week in the summer, and since you don't really know anybody in Nowthen...well, I just hated to think of you sitting alone in the hotel when the rest of the town is out having such a good time..."

"That's really very nice of you, Mrs. Harmon, but..."

"I'd really appreciate the company," Elaine interrupted quietly. "Franklin and I always go to these things together, but of course he won't be home until tomorrow morning.''

Frances sighed and pushed herself up to lean back on the headboard. ''I'll need a few minutes to get ready...''

''Wonderful!'' The voice brightened considerably—almost too much, Frances thought, as if luring her out of the hotel room had been an assignment of some sort, now successfully completed. ''I'll be waiting. Wear something casual, now.''

Frances replaced the receiver thoughtfully, unable to shake the feeling that she'd just been had in some way. Finally she shrugged and hopped out of bed, discounting the notion. City living had made her cynical, that was all, almost paranoid, looking for ulterior motives behind every simple gesture of kindness. Elaine Harmon was just one of those incredibly thoughtful women with the welfare of others uppermost in her mind—and obviously she was just a bit lonely tonight too. There was no more to the supper invitation than that.

She stretched and yawned, expecting to be groggy and sluggish, a little surprised to find she felt wonderfully refreshed and full of energy. All that pre-nap anxiety about somehow losing her identity in this town seemed a little silly now, with a few hours of sleep behind her. She'd just been tired, that was all, and when you were tired you overreacted.

She peeled off the sleep-wrinkled suit and pulled an equally wrinkled silk skirt and blouse from the jumble of her suitcase. Shaking her head at her earlier foolishness, she told herself she was the same person she was when she had first driven into this town only yesterday. Yes, she'd been touched by a wounded calf and horrified by the ravages of fire and moved by her perfectly natural response to a man's skilled seduction—but none of that had really changed her. Frances Katharine Hudson was still intact, still in control, still mistress of her own destiny.

Even wrinkled, the emerald silk blouse draped beautifully from her shoulders, and the matching skirt seemed to slide from her shapely indented waist over her hips like a waterfall. It wasn't exactly casual, but it was less rigid than one of her suits. She smiled at her reflection as she brushed her hair into shiny waves, telling herself again that she hadn't changed a bit, then she went downstairs to join Elaine.

In the silent, empty room, glinting in the afternoon sunlight streaming through the window, the pins she always used to clamp down her hair lay forgotten on the top of the dresser.

"They're not exactly the Philharmonic, are they?" Elaine chuckled.

The two of them were sitting on a park bench facing the bandstand, listening to the Nowthen Senior Citizens' Band. They were playing an enthusiastic, if slightly off-key rendition of a familiar march.

"Maybe not," Frances replied, smiling at a wiry old-timer bobbing in time to the bellows of his tuba, "but then I don't think the Philharmonic has half the fun they do either."

Elaine smiled at the reply, and Frances had the feeling that she'd said precisely the right thing. She sighed and leaned against the back of the bench, an alien figure in this crowd of blue jeans and T-shirts, yet not feeling alienated at all. Elaine had been responsible for that, of course. She'd paraded Frances through the food lines like a mother hen herding a chick, introducing her to more people in a single half hour than Frances had met in the past six years, and she'd introduced her to every one of them as "Frannie"—not Frances Hudson, insurance investigator for Northeastern Casualty—just Frannie. After a while, no one noticed that her emerald silk outfit was better suited to a Boston club than a small-town park; and, after a while, Frances didn't notice it either.

She'd had two beers—frosty bottles served from a tub filled with ice—two hot dogs on homemade buns so warm that she could still feel the heat on her lips, and now she was trying to lick a mound of ice cream down into the cone before it melted all over her fingers.

Elaine was facing her on the bench, her dark eyes alight, her little mouth quirked in a smile.

She had a full, matronly figure that shouldn't have looked good in jeans and a tucked-in shirt, but did anyway. "Thanks for keeping me company tonight, Frannie. Franklin was afraid I'd stay home by myself and mope without him, and I think I might have if you hadn't agreed to come with me. And you're having a good time too, aren't you?"

Frances hesitated for a moment, a little surprised to realize that she was. "Yes," she said, grinning helplessly, "I am." She swiped at the mound of melting ice cream with her tongue as she looked around her.

The cool promise of evening was settling over the lush green of the park, welcome relief from the unseasonable heat of the day. A setting sun striped the grass with long shadows, the tree leaves whispered in a light breeze, trying to be heard over the happy noise of a community of friends coming together. There were no gowns here, no celebrities, and the Nowthen Senior Citizens' Band was about as far removed from a symphony orchestra as it could get—and yet Frances was having a good time. Somehow that seemed remarkable.

"Oh, there's Beth!" Elaine said suddenly, jumping up from the bench. "I'll have to talk to her for just a minute . . . you don't mind, do you, dear?" And then she was gone before Frances had a chance to reply.

She was staring after her, mystified by such a hasty departure, when suddenly someone moved from behind the bench to take Elaine's seat. She turned her head, cone held at the ready before her mouth, and looked up into blue eyes that seemed iridescent under the sun's last rays.

Ethan's mouth twitched slightly, as if he was enjoying a private joke, and Frances was visibly relieved when he turned his head to look out over the park. "Not exactly the night life you're used to, is it?" he remarked.

She cleared her throat quietly. "Not exactly."

He nodded, his eyes fixed on a trio of children soaring on a distant set of swings. "Let's see," he mused, "it's the second Tuesday in June. What would you be doing in Boston? The Pops? The Chamber Orchestra? The ballet?"

"Well, I . . . how do you know so much about what goes on in Boston?"

He looked straight at her, but ignored her question. "Your calf is better, by the way."

"Oh." A smile came from nowhere, softening her face, lightening her eyes. "I'm glad."

He answered her smile with one of his own. "You have eyes like a cat's, you know that?"

Her smile faltered in confusion. He was jumping from subject to subject too fast, leaving her behind. She felt the color rising up her neck to her face, and she turned her head quickly to face front. An after image of what he looked like, smiling at her like that, flashed behind her eyes as if her mind had taken a photograph.

Blue denim shirt, sleeves rolled to the elbow, faded jeans painted over muscular thighs, the white of his smile flashing in the tan of his face, the aging sun dancing in his light hair...she had to blink a few times to get rid of the picture.

"And you aren't wearing a suit."

She could tell from his voice that he was still looking at her, and the color in her face deepened.

"And..." she shivered when his fingers rasped together over a curl of her hair, less than an inch from her shoulder "...you've set your hair free. Lord, it's beautiful! Why on earth would a woman with hair like this try to keep it hidden?"

She'd frozen the moment he had reached for her hair, almost afraid to breathe, certain that every single man, woman and child in the park knew what was happening on this bench.

"So," Ethan went on in a soft murmur, "no suit, no bun, an ice-cream cone in your hand, and I'll bet if I kissed you I'd taste hot dog."

Her eyes flew wide and she jumped to her feet, unable to control the desperate instinct to flee.

"Frannie," he said softly behind her, "you're still running."

She froze in mid-stride, and the moment elongated. She felt the silken brush of her skirt against the backs of her knees, smelled the mingling aromas of grilling hot dogs and freshly cut grass, heard the sleepy chirp of a bird settling in a branch overhead. These were ordinary things; nothing to be afraid of, nothing to run from. She willed herself to be calm and sank back onto the bench, her feet aligned perfectly, her hands folded in her lap. "I'm not running," she said steadily, her eyes fixed forward.

"Good. I'd hate to think you were afraid of me."

"I'm not."

His soft, disbelieving chuckle stung more than she would have thought possible. "Maybe not me, Frannie; but something. You're sure as hell afraid of something. Your own feelings, maybe, because every time I touch you..." he pressed a single finger down on her shoulder and she jumped involuntarily "...you do that."

Frances felt her lower lip quiver in frustration because he read her too well, and too easily. "You make me nervous," she said lamely, "not afraid."

She couldn't explain the impulse; she didn't even understand it; but suddenly, for the first time in her life, she wanted someone to know just who she was, what she had been through, how much she had accomplished. Afraid? Sure, she'd been afraid, lots of times. Afraid that she'd be trapped in the vicious circle of poverty that had consumed the best years of her mother's life; afraid that one day she'd be recognized as little Frannie Hudson from the tenements, and be rejected because of it. But the fear had left her the day she had boarded the crosstown bus for her new job in Northeastern Casualty's glass and steel tower downtown. After she'd made it through that day—after she'd learned that people accepted the image you presented and never even bothered to look for the real person beneath— she had never been afraid again. Until now.

Image. Image was everything, she reminded herself. Concentrate on the image you present, and eventually you'll *become* that image.

She turned her head slowly to look at Ethan and although what he saw was a strangely childlike woman with hair spilling over her shoulders and ice cream dripping from a cone on to her hand, inside she was the woman who had come to town in a designer suit with her hair coiled tightly into a bun. Inside, her image was back in place. "I should find Elaine," she said. "It's time I was leaving."

"Elaine left a long time ago," he told her.

"She wouldn't do that. We came together."

"She knows you're with me. That's why she brought you here."

Frances gaped at him, astonished. "And whose idea was that?"

He smiled and shrugged. "Does it matter?"

She knew she should have said something— anything—but no words came to mind.

"Topaz," he murmured, gazing into her eyes. "That's what color they are. I don't think I've ever seen eyes quite like yours."

She had to force herself not to slam the damn things shut, just to keep him from commenting on them. What kind of a thing was that to say?

"Here, you're making a mess. Let me take that." Gently, like a parent taking a treasured toy from a child, Ethan removed the cone from her hand and tossed it into the litter basket next to the bench. Frances gazed down at the drops of ice cream on her fingers, wondering how they had got there without her noticing.

She risked a glance in his direction, but he wasn't looking at her.

"Miles." He nodded at the man approaching the bench with a beer in each hand. Clean trousers and a shirt had replaced the grimy overalls, but Frances recognized him as the man at the gas station.

"Ethan." He nodded back, and then to her, "Ma'am." He handed them each a frosty bottle.

Frances accepted with her clean hand, holding the other out awkwardly to keep the ice cream from dripping on her dress. Miles grabbed the sticky hand and shook it before she could stop him. She blushed at his expression when he gazed down at his own sticky palm.

"Ice cream," she explained, embarrassed.

"Yep," Miles said, pulling a folded handkerchief from his pocket and handing it to her.

"Have you met Miss Hudson, Miles?" Ethan asked.

"Yep," Miles replied.

"Frannie," Frances murmured without thinking, staring down at the neatly folded handkerchief.

"Frannie," he repeated. "Nice to see you again." Then he left without another word.

Heavens, she thought, had she really said that? Had she really identified herself as Frannie? She turned to look at him, confusion rounding the almond shape of her eyes before she could think to conceal it. "Why did he do that?" she asked, trying to divert his attention from her own uncertainty.

He smiled as if he could see through the question to the muddle of her feelings. "Why did he do what?"

"Bring us beer—give me his hankie——"

"It's a small town," Ethan said simply, as if that was an answer in itself.

"But I'm a stranger here."

"Yesterday you were a stranger. But that was yesterday." He grabbed her hand as if it were the most natural thing in the world to do. "Come on—you've had a busy day. I'll walk you to the hotel."

Without ever thinking to object, she allowed herself to be led through the thinning crowd, past the whitewashed bandstand, out on to the relative quiet of the street. The streetlights spilled golden circles onto a pavement that bore the colorful chalk marks of a child's game. A muted, melodic chorus of chirps seemed to keep time to their footsteps. It was a pretty noise, and it made her smile. "What's that sound?" she asked.

"Peepers—toads, frogs, crickets—country sounds."

For the three blocks to the hotel, Frances kept pace with Ethan's longer strides, soothed by the tranquillity of a small town at night, barely aware that her hand was still encased by his. It was almost as if she were alone, until suddenly they were standing before her hotel room door and Ethan released her hand. Later, she would think how odd it was that she noticed his presence not when she could feel the touch of his hand, but when she couldn't. Suddenly the situation became very awkward.

She turned to face him, found herself too close, and stepped backward until she thumped into the door. Embarrassed, she blinked hard, then spoke quickly to cover the sudden, oppressive feeling that she was trapped. "Er—well, thank you. Thank you for walking me home." Her mouth twitched in a weak smile.

Silence for the space of a heartbeat, and then, "Look at me, Frannie."

For a moment, unblinking, she continued to stare at the expanse of blue denim at eye level.

"Frannie."

Her thoughts fluttered and scrambled and bumped into one another. Get out of here, Frances, they said. Turn your back and dive into that room and slam and lock the door behind you, because if you don't, you'll regret it for the rest of your life. And for pity's sake, whatever you do, don't look into his eyes.

Slowly, hesitantly, she lifted her chin and met Ethan's gaze.

The blue of his eyes seemed to blossom like the nova of a dying star, sparks shooting outward with the force of an explosion, then whirling back to fiery pinpoints of light. Frances felt herself being drawn into the center of that light like a scrap of paper caught in the spinning funnel of a firestorm. The blue eyes moved closer and closer, and by the time Frances thought to break away, his arms were braced against the door on either side of her head and his lips were trembling against hers.

A sudden roaring noise filled her ears like the thunder of a roller coaster rushing down from its last peak, and she was a passenger on that roller coaster, feeling the wind pressing against her, flattening her breasts, snatching the air from her mouth before she could draw it into her lungs. Terrified and exhilarated, she let herself be swept away, helpless to do otherwise, then suddenly, cruelly, the ride was over.

"Good night, Frannie," Ethan murmured against her mouth, and by the time she opened her eyes she found herself trembling against the door, searching the shadows of the hall, totally alone. Again.

CHAPTER FIVE

FRANCES sat at the Harmons' kitchen table, a partially completed claim form weighted down by a mug of steaming coffee. Elaine was bustling from counter to oven, monitoring the baking of fresh cinnamon rolls while Franklin answered Frannie's questions. He was a burly, muscular man with a kind face and a gruff, no-nonsense voice. Frances had liked him on sight. His hands were loosely wrapped in white gauze to protect his burns, but just imagining what lay beneath the bandages made Frances cringe.

"So you never heard the smoke alarms?" she asked, still scribbling his last answer.

"Nope. And if you want my opinion, the damn things never went off. We had them wired to an intercom in the bedroom, you know, just in case something like this ever happened, but neither one of us heard a thing until Blackie started to bawl."

"Blackie?"

"The bull," Elaine put in quietly, glancing worriedly at her husband's strained expression. Clearly the loss of the bull had affected Franklin as much as it had his wife. "Does it matter if the alarm worked or not?"

"We might have a cause of action against the manufacturer if there was a mechanical failure," Frances explained. "Obviously you did everything you could to protect your property. Installing the alarms, the intercom..." Her gaze drifted to his bandaged hands and she marveled again at the kind of courage it would take to dive into a burning building to save an animal.

Franklin cleared his throat, but his voice still cracked when he tried to talk. "I just...couldn't save them."

Frances looked down, her lips pursed hard, pretending not to notice the strong man's attempt to contain his grief. And it *was* grief—for a bunch of dumb animals. Frances found that nearly impossible to understand. "Well," she said with forced brightness, laying down her pen, "I think that's all I need for now."

"That's all there is to it?" asked Franklin, swiping at his eyes with his beefy forearm.

"Your job is done, except for your signature on the final copy of the claim form. I still need the veterinary records, a value appraisal, and a report from the fire department, but I won't have to bother you for any of those things."

"You could never be a bother, Frannie," Elaine said kindly. "As a matter of fact, if there's anything good to come from this nightmare, it's been meeting you."

"Oh, well." Frances's lips quivered in a tremulous smile. "What a nice thing to say.

Thank you." The words were proper, almost stilted, but she had to blink rapidly as she said them. "I really should be going now." The chair legs scraped angrily against the tile floor as she rose to her feet.

"Nonsense," Elaine said quickly. "You haven't had breakfast yet, and, besides, Ethan won't be here for another hour."

Frances blanched. Were her feelings so obvious that even Elaine could see them? "Ethan? I don't need to see Ethan. What made you think I wanted to see Ethan?"

Franklin's bushy salt and pepper brows quirked in a puzzled frown. "You did say you'd need his records, didn't you?"

"Oh." She blushed furiously. "Yes, of course. It's just that I don't need to see him this morning. Actually, I don't need to see him at all—just his records. I can just go to his office, ask for the files, maybe you could call his secretary and arrange for me to see them..." She knew she was babbling, she could see the puzzled amusement on the Harmons' faces, and yet she couldn't make herself stop until Elaine interrupted her.

"Ethan doesn't have a secretary," she said gently, "or an office, for that matter. He works out of his house, and he'll have to unlock the files for you."

"Oh." Frances felt as if she'd been punched in the stomach.

"But if you're in a hurry I'll tell him to call you later at the hotel."

"Oh, good. Wonderful! That's just fine. Thank you." Frances felt a giggle building somewhere deep inside—a helpless, hysterical reaction to her inexplicable, idiotic behavior—and knew she had to get out of the house before the giggle escaped. She was a blur of motion moving from the table to the back door, and then with a cursory wave, she fled outside, leaving Franklin and Elaine staring after her, mystified.

That bizarre sense of impending hysteria vanished the moment she found herself alone in the barnyard. Nothing was ever funny when you were alone, she thought, and she felt very alone at this moment. The yard looked deserted, abandoned, and it occurred to her that this was the first time she'd been here without Ethan. Was that why the place looked so empty? Simply because he wasn't in it?

She shrugged away the notion with an angry jerk of her shoulders and walked toward her car. Halfway there she heard the muted bleat of the calf coming from the little white building, as if it were calling her. A smile touched her lips as she glanced down ruefully at her white trousers. Ruining clothes was getting to be a habit!

"Hey, little girl," she said softly as she entered the cool shadows of the barn, squinting to adjust her eyes.

"Yes? What is it?" came the reply from the stall, as if the calf had answered her. Frances gasped and clutched her heart.

"Who's there?" she whispered fearfully.

A figure rose from the darkness of the distant stall, and Frances approached cautiously.

"Hi," the figure said cheerfully. "You're Frannie, aren't you?"

"Ye-es." She stopped at the stall entrance, her eyes finally adjusting to the gloom.

A young, fresh face gleamed in the dim light, and Frances felt a sharp, nostalgic tug at her consciousness. What would it be like, she wondered, to be so young, so trusting, so in love with the world that it shone outward from your face like that?

The girl was beautiful—a tiny, tomboyish figure with a gaminelike face dominated by dark, thickly lashed eyes. Her hair was shiny black, cropped close to her head. She stood next to the calf, one perfectly formed hand resting on the creature's bony head.

"I'm Beth," she said, "Ethan's assistant. I saw you at the park last night, and I wanted to come over then and introduce myself..." her features clouded slightly "...but Elaine said I should wait."

The calf interrupted with a soft lowing, its neck stretched toward Frances, its eyes half closed. Beth looked down and giggled. "I think you'd better come and say hello, before she tries to come to you.''

Frances took a step into the stall, her hand outstretched. The calf's broad, sleek tongue swiped at her hand, making the hairs on the back of her neck stand up.

''Ethan was right,'' Beth said with a smile. ''That calf is purely in love with you.''

Frances laughed nervously, enthralled by the calf's obvious affection. She knelt next to it on the mats, eyeing the IV needle still firmly embedded in its leg. ''When can you take the IV out?'' she asked.

Beth knelt down, absently scratching the calf's ear. ''Actually, it should have come out yesterday. She's drinking now, so there's no more danger of dehydration, but her pulse is still fast, almost shocky, and she's not taking the bottle well. She lost her mother in the fire, you know, and the shift to bottled milk from mother's milk is always an adjustment, without the added trauma of her burns.''

Frances looked up at the girl, impressed by her knowledge. ''Are you a vet too?''

Beth laughed merrily. ''Good heavens, no! I just do what Ethan tells me, and pick up a little know-how along the way.''

''It sounds like more than 'a little know-how' to me. You should be going to college, becoming a vet yourself. Elaine said you really had a way with animals."

Beth shrugged. "I love animals, always have. But I sure don't want to waste six years of my life in college."

"Waste?" Frances gasped. "How can you say that? You have a talent for this, a gift. You're wasting that, by not using it."

Beth frowned and smiled all at the same time. "But I *am* using it."

"But you're just an assistant. You could be so much more."

"The only thing more I want to be is a wife..." her cheeks colored prettily "...and, eventually, a mother."

Frances gaped at her, baffled by her simplistic goals. All her life she had fought to have more than the traditional role assigned to most women. Meeting someone who *aspired* to such a role was almost beyond her comprehension. "You've never wanted more than that?" she whispered.

Beth shrugged and smiled. "Maybe if I'd been born to it like Ethan, I'd want the money, the career, the clothes...all that. But growing up in a place like this gives you a whole different perspective, I think." She paused, head cocked as she puzzled over something.

Frances had frozen, her hand motionless on the calf's neck, her eyes fixed on Beth's face. "What do you mean, born to it like Ethan?" she asked woodenly.

"You know—silver spoon and all that—servants, money, high society..."

"Ethan?" Frances whispered.

Beth glanced up, then did a double take at Frances's incredulous expression. "Oh, I suppose you wouldn't have any way of knowing that, would you? He never talks about his family." She paused and chuckled. "And, from what I gather, they never talk about him. He's been the black sheep ever since he left med school in Boston. They can't stand it that all he ever wanted to be was a country vet."

Flabbergasted, Frances murmured, "That's remarkable. I didn't know that about him."

"Ethan is a very remarkable man."

Frances looked down when the calf butted her hand impatiently, liquid eyes rolling back in mute reprimand for her neglect. Compelled by an impulse she would never understand, she wrapped both arms around the calf's neck and pressed her cheek to the top of its head. "There, there, baby," she murmured, freely giving the calf a part of herself she had never been able to give a human being, "it's all right. Everything's going to be all right."

"You really love that calf, don't you?" Beth asked tenderly.

Frances didn't say anything for a moment, considering the question. "I'm growing fond of her," she said at last.

She caught herself smiling on the drive back into town after talking with Beth. Aside from her being just plain likable, there was something so right about the girl, something that made you feel good just being around her. She was pretty, of course, and bright—the kind of young woman who could have the world for the taking—and yet her real charm was that she didn't want the world; she just wanted her own small place in it.

Beth and I are really very much alike, Frances thought. The things we want from life are different, of course; but we've both always known what those things were, and we've never strayed from the paths we chose to get them.

She sighed, wondering what it might have been like to be Beth, to grow up in a place like Nowthen, where everyone was a neighbor, and all your neighbors were friends. Maybe her own choices would have been different, if she'd had a father who hadn't died before her first birthday; a childhood that hadn't centered on the simple struggle to stay alive. Maybe it was easy to be an optimist, to believe in the basic goodness of life and people, when life and people had always been good to you.

She stopped that train of thought before it could go any further. She had learned a long time ago that you couldn't change the past, and crying about the way things had been never altered the way things would be. Only work did that; work, determination, and sometimes just sheer force of will. Frances had never lacked for any of those...until she'd met Ethan Alexander, that was. She certainly hadn't displayed much force of will when he'd kissed her in the barn, and then again at her hotel room door. As a matter of fact, she hadn't displayed much of anything except an embarrassing inability to control her own responses—something that had never happened to her before. She had been pursued by the wealthy, the sophisticated, the urbane; and yet none of these men had moved her the way the simple country vet had.

But he's not just a simple country vet, she reminded herself. On the contrary, he was turning out to be a mysterious, complicated man with a past as full of secrets as her own. He'd come from the kind of place she had always been trying to go, and yet apparently he had turned his back on it voluntarily. What would possess someone to do such a thing? She pondered the question until she got back to the hotel. Margaret was dusting the lobby desk when she walked in.

"Well, look at you!" She paused in her work and pushed her fists into the comfortable rolls above her gingham apron. "Every time you leave this place you come back looking like you've been rolling in a barnyard! Don't you think it's about time you bought some clothes fit for whatever it is you're doing around here?"

Frances glanced down at the streaks of dust on her white trousers, and gave Margaret a small smile and shrug. "Where do I go and what do I buy?" she asked.

"I'll go with you," said Margaret, trying to sound gruff. She untied her apron and laid it on the registration desk. "You're going to need some help if you want to look like you belong in this town."

Frances followed her broad form out of the door, smiling, feeling a little as if she already belonged.

CHAPTER SIX

THE woman in the mirror looked ridiculous. Frances made a face at her reflection, thinking she looked just as silly in a tartan shirt and jeans as Margaret would in a tailored suit. She wiggled her toes in the stiff canvas of brand-new tennis shoes, peering down at them through the curtain of hair. Even her feet looked ridiculous, she decided. She couldn't possibly go out in public dressed like this. She didn't care how many suits she ruined at the Harmon farm.

She panicked for a moment at the sudden rap on the door, then remembered Margaret was bringing fresh towels. "Come on in, Margaret," she called without looking around. "You're the one who picked this outfit; you might as well get the first laugh." She parodied a model's turn toward the door—then froze.

Ethan was standing there, one light brow arched in amusement. He wore a one-piece overall reminiscent of hospital whites, and his face looked haggard. Slowly, insolently, his gaze traveled from the rounded toes of her tennis shoes upward, stuttering to a sudden halt at where the shirt clung to the soft swell of her breasts. Frances felt the heat rise to her face.

"Better. Much, much better." His eyes lightened to blue frost and held her transfixed.

"It was Margaret's idea," she murmured tonelessly, staring at him, unable to take her eyes from his. She wasn't aware of his reaching back to close the door, but the sound of the latch clicking shut startled her out of her trance. "I—I was ruining all my clothes out at the farm," she stammered.

One side of his mouth curled in a smile. "It happens all the time." He gestured down at his own soiled overalls. "I just came from a barn call."

"So," she shrugged nervously. "Is there something wrong? Why are you here...?" Her face stilled suddenly and she caught her breath. "The calf...?"

"The calf is fine." He continued to stare at her.

"Oh. Good." She took a breath and pressed her lips together, wondering what to say next.

"Elaine told me you needed to see my records."

Frances nodded, relieved that he had a reason for coming...and then, a moment later, disappointed that he had a reason for coming.

"So let's go," he added.

She frowned, wishing he wouldn't keep staring at her so intently, as if this awkward conversation had a good deal more import than the words implied. "I was just about to go downstairs for supper..."

"We'll eat at my place. I'll cook."

She smiled a little, her thoughts scrambling for a reason not to go, convinced that she shouldn't go, that there was a very real danger in going... "Wonderful," her lips said before she could stop them. "Just give me a minute to change."

"Into what?"

"Into something... more suitable than this." She gestured lamely at her clothes.

Ethan smiled a little, and the line that ran from his eyes to hers seemed to crackle with repressed energy. "What you're wearing is fine, Frannie. Perfect, in fact." His hand swept up and back to brush a few strands of wayward fair hair from his brow, and for some reason she found the gesture mesmerizing.

Later, as she followed a few lengths behind his pickup in her sedan, it occurred to her that she would have gone with him dressed in an old feed sack, if he'd said that was perfect; that she'd never really had a choice of whether or not to go with him, or what she would wear. Somehow, on a subconscious level, she had relinquished control, and the odd thing was that knowing she had done that didn't frighten her any more.

A few miles east of town he turned on to a dirt road, and then to the right at a carved wooden sign that read "Ethan Alexander, D.V.M." Frances had expected that, since his office was in his home, the location would be on a main road somewhere, easily accessible to the public; but the lane that served as his driveway was so narrow that it was almost intimidating. Trees crowded either side, occasionally brushing against her car as she followed his truck up a steady, gradual incline. The surrounding woods were so thick that only a dappling of sunlight peppered the ferns beneath. She felt as if she was on a little-used trail to someone's secret hideaway; a trail made purposely difficult to discourage visitors.

The lane ended in a large, sunny clearing that opened on to a spectacular view of New Hampshire's White Mountains marching away to the north. A sprawling log house sat on the clearing's highest point facing the mountains, and appeared at first to be poised on the brink of the edge of the world. The soaring, jumbled roof-lines of the different sections of the house cut sharp angles into the blue sky, and every polished window mirrored the scenery it faced.

He was out of his truck first, his eyes watching her face as she climbed out of her car and turned in a slow circle, looking at the woods, the distant mountains, and then the house itself. In a brief flash of perception, she realized that this was Ethan Alexander's hiding place. Just as she hid in her fashionable town house from the poor neighborhood that had produced her, Ethan hid here, in these miles of emptiness, from the place and the life he had left behind.

"This is about as far from your beginnings as you could get, isn't it?" she asked quietly, looking him straight in the eye.

He flinched slightly. "You've been investigating a little more than Franklin's fire, haven't you?"

She shook her head, shivering when the motion lifted the hair slightly from the nape of her neck. "Not intentionally. I met Beth this morning, and she told me a little about you."

He nodded once and looked off into the distance. "How much?"

"Not nearly enough." The words were out of her mouth before she knew she was going to say them, and he smiled at her startled expression.

"Come on, Frannie." He took her hand so casually that it never occurred to her to resist, and led her to a small side door. "The front entrance leads into the office. This one is private," he explained. A small entryway opened on to a large kitchen, warmed by log walls and hanging copper pots, brightened by a skylight.

"Take a stool at the breakfast bar," said Ethan. "We'll have some wine first, then I'll shower while you look at the records."

The wine was an excellent, smooth Beaujolais—the kind that went down much too easily, particularly when your attention was focused elsewhere... like on a pair of brilliant blue eyes facing yours across a narrow expanse of countertop.

"This is very good," Frances said, more to fill the silence than to compliment his choice of wine, taking another sip too soon after the last one.

She glanced at the bottle between them, her brows lifting at the label. "You have wine like this every night?"

"Absolutely not."

"Oh." She sipped again, wishing she hadn't asked, because his answer gave too much importance to her presence here. She'd just pretend she hadn't asked and he hadn't answered, and then she wouldn't have to acknowledge...

"This is your first time here. The wine is a celebration."

She smiled nervously, anxious to change the subject. "How long have you lived in Nowthen?"

"Eight years. I came here straight out of vet school."

"Beth said you were in med school——"

"I dropped out," he interrupted. "Much to my father's dismay."

She raised her brows in a silent question, and Ethan sighed.

"My father's a doctor, my grandfather was a doctor, and his father before him...I was the first Alexander son to break tradition. They don't forgive you for something like that in my family."

"But you said yourself, you *are* a doctor."

He shook his head with a bitter smile. "In my family, a doctor wears a three-piece suit, a monogrammed stethoscope, and golfs at the club every Wednesday afternoon."

"You could have been a different kind of doctor, the kind who really cares about the people he treats."

"The thing is, I didn't like people much in those days. The only ones I knew were just like my father—superficial, obsessed with image, intent on amassing the symbols of material wealth..." He shrugged helplessly, and Frances sat in numb silence, thinking that he had just described her.

"There's nothing wrong with trying to better yourself," she said quietly.

"Of course there isn't. Until the symbols of wealth become more important than the things that really matter."

"Like...?"

He sipped his wine, eyeing her reflectively over his glass. "Like relationships."

Frances looked away. The conversation was getting too uncomfortable, too intense.

"I think it's about time I showered before supper," he said quietly, perhaps noticing her discomfort. "I'll get you settled in the office first."

He led her down a hallway to a small office crowded with filing cabinets, placed the Harmon files on the desk in front of her and then left. It was hard for Frances to concentrate on her work, maybe because of the wine, maybe because the sound of the shower in a distant room was distracting. All she needed for her report were some simple statistics about the animals which had died, but she couldn't seem to focus her attention on the file.

Little unfamiliar noises kept disturbing her train of thought—the gentle ticking of a wall clock, the chatter of birds outside the window, and the faint scratching at the door behind her...

She turned her ear to the door and cocked her head, listening. There it was again. Something small, something quiet, perhaps a pet inadvertently locked in a closet.

Quietly she left her chair to open the door a crack, peeped around it, then felt all the air leave her body in a rush as the door slammed against her chest.

A snarling mass of black and tan vaulted into the room and spun to face her from the other side of the desk, head lowered menacingly, a growl vibrating deep in its throat.

Paralyzed, Frances gaped wide-eyed at where the German shepherd's lip lifted away from large white teeth. Oh, my God—oh, my God, her thoughts clattered against the closed door of her mind while her mouth worked silently. She wanted to scream, but she couldn't find her voice. She wanted to run, but some long-buried instinct kept her frozen in place. The only sounds in the small room were the sporadic snarling of the dog and the deafening pounding of her own heart.

"Ethan," she finally managed to whisper, watching the dog for a reaction to her voice. If it attacked, she'd dash into the room where the dog had been locked and slam the door behind her—if it didn't get to her first. The dog remained motionless, its head still lowered, hackles raised. "Ethan," she said a little louder, and still the dog did nothing. She decided to risk a step toward the door, but the moment she moved, the dog lunged forward a step and barked.

Frances couldn't help herself. She screamed, and once started, she couldn't stop. The office reverberated with the sounds of the dog's frantic barking and her piercing screams.

She stopped screaming when Ethan raced into the room, dripping from the shower, clutching a towel to his waist. He froze just inside the doorway, his eyes darting from Frances to the dog, then back again. "Don't move, Frannie," he commanded quietly, then all his attention was focused on the dog. He dropped to one knee, extended a hand palm up, and spoke softly. "Hey, girl, it's okay. No one's going to hurt you. Come on, girl. Come on over here, Frances..."

"*Frances*? Your dog's name is *Frances*?"

He silenced her with a quick, hard scowl, then continued to talk to the dog in a soothing tone. "Come on, girl—that's right. Come right to me."

Frances watched warily as the dog took a few stiff-legged steps toward Ethan, its head still lowered. It's going to kill him, she thought. It's going to kill him first and then it's going to kill me, and then it will probably eat us both.

It seemed to take forever for the dog to cross the small room to Ethan's waiting hand, and Frances held her breath, waiting for the vicious beast to lunge out and sink its teeth into his palm. Instead, the sculpted head dropped slightly in submission, and the dog whined softly.

Frances sagged against the wall, her knees weak with relief.

"That's my girl," murmured Ethan, slipping the fingers of one hand beneath the dog's collar while he stroked her head with the other. "She's a stray," he explained without looking up. "And, from the looks of her when she showed up here a few days ago, she'd been on the road for a long time, fending for herself. She took a few good kicks from someone along the way. There were bruises here, and here." He pointed to two places on her rib cage.

Frances shook her head wildly from side to side, stopped when the dog's head spun to pinpoint the sudden motion. "She's a killer," she whispered. "She was going to kill me. You should have seen the way she shot out of that room, pinned me behind the desk, growling..."

Ethan closed his eyes briefly. "If you'd so much as raised your voice to her, she probably would have run for cover, her tail between her legs. You scared her, that's all. No one's ever opened that door for her but me."

Frances gaped at him. "Are you out of your mind?" she demanded. "I didn't scare her. I tell you she was going to attack!"

He pressed his lips together and frowned. "I hope you're wrong about that. I'd hate to have to put her down."

"Put her down?"

He nodded grimly. "Put her to sleep. Kill her. It's what I'll have to do if it turns out she's so afraid of people she can't be trusted."

Frances hesitated, frowning. "But you're a vet! You're not supposed to kill animals. You're supposed to save them."

His shoulders moved in a silent, bitter chuckle. "In a perfect world, that's what a vet does. But an imperfect world creates people who mistreat animals, and sometimes, when they've been treated badly enough for long enough, they assume everyone is an enemy." He looked up at her again, and she saw something soft and warm in his eyes. "They're not really so different from us, are they?"

She pressed her lips together, not knowing what to say.

He rose to his feet with a sigh. "Come on, Frances. Time to go back to your room. Maybe you and Frannie can get to know each other another time."

Frances backed quickly away from the door, never taking her eyes from the dog as Ethan led her to the doorway, then urged her through. She didn't completely relax until he'd closed the door behind her; then she had to brace herself on the wall to keep from collapsing in a heap. Her knees were still shaking.

"Frannie." The towel slipped on his waist and his hands snatched at it, fastening it more securely. "I'm sorry she frightened you."

"You said she was a stray. When did she get here?"

He pretended to think about that. "Let me see. A few days ago, I guess . . ."

"The day I arrived?" she persisted, and he tried to suppress a smile.

"Maybe. Could be."

"You named that dog after me, didn't you?" she accused him, her lower lip jutting out.

He finally surrendered to the smile, and it made him look infuriatingly boyish. "You were both new in town. It seemed appropriate."

Frances exhaled in noisy exasperation and he chuckled. "When you're finished in here, come back to the kitchen. We'll make supper together."

"Together?"

"Consider it a trial run."

"For what?"

"For whatever you like, Frannie."

CHAPTER SEVEN

FRANCES worked rapidly in the little office, jumping at the slightest sound from the room behind the desk. It's a sturdy door, she kept telling herself; there's no way that dog is going to get out. Still, she could hardly wait to get out of the room. Even with the door between them, the dog was too close to suit her.

Finally she closed the files, winced when the old leather chair squeaked as she got up, and tiptoed out into the hall, holding her breath. She retraced her steps quickly, quietly back to the kitchen, then stopped in the doorway.

Ethan was busy at the counter, his back to her, dressed now in loose black pants and a billowing white shirt that reminded her of a pirate movie she'd seen as a girl. She watched him for a moment without making a sound. He was chopping something on a long cutting board with the practiced movements of a master chef. She saw the interplay of his shoulder muscles beneath the thin fabric of the shirt, the quiver of his hair that matched the chopping sounds of the knife—and then he stilled suddenly, raised his head, and looked over his shoulder.

"Hi. Did you get everything you needed from the files?"

She actually *felt* his smile, like the steady push of a strong hand on her chest. She nodded mutely, then felt a rush of blood to her face when his eyes raced up and down her body. There was nothing really lascivious about his expression, nothing insulting; it was more like a friendly appraisal. Still, it made her painfully aware of what she was wearing. She wasn't used to the heavy cling of denim circling her legs, to the constraint of a snug blouse pressing against her breasts, to *any* clothing that outlined her body so immodestly.

A nervous smile flickered across her face. "You have appraisals on all the Harmon cattle in your files. I'd like copies of the sheets on the cows he lost, if possible. I'll need something stating their value before I can file the claim."

He nodded absently, meeting her gaze. "No problem. I'll get them to you tomorrow."

Frances felt a sharp pain in her hands, and looked down to see she was clasping them so tightly together that the skin under her fingertips was turning white.

"I poured you another glass of wine."

She followed his glance to the snack bar, then rushed over to pick up her glass, enormously grateful for any diversion. She took a sip, and only looked up when she heard his knife at work again.

"Why don't you start chopping the celery while I work on the rest of this?" he said without looking up.

A bunch of celery lay a few feet down from him at the cutting board, a wicked-looking knife next to it. Frances eyed the glinting blade doubtfully and wiped her palms on the sides of her jeans as she approached. "How do you want it cut?"

"Bite-size is fine. Hope you like stir-fry."

Frances hesitated, picked up the knife gingerly, then began slicing the leafy green stalks with elaborate care. So great was her concentration that she didn't notice Ethan watching her out of the corner of his eye, trying to suppress a smile.

This isn't so bad, she thought after a time, watching the little green crescents fall like a row of dominoes under her knife. She couldn't remember the last time she'd actually prepared a meal. She rarely ate at home, and, when she did, it was usually a boxed dinner that went directly from freezer to oven—a practice that horrified her mother. The creation of meals had always been an expression of love in the little apartment, and Frances smiled wistfully, remembering the ones they had prepared together. Those had been the best of times, those hours in the tiny, fragrant kitchen, her mother humming constantly under her breath.

Still looking down at his work, Ethan smiled when he heard her start to hum. "You like to cook, don't you?"

She cocked her head, knife poised for another stroke, and thought about that for a moment. "I used to," she said finally. "When I still lived with my mother. I haven't done much cooking since."

"It's no fun alone," he sighed, eyes intent on the flash of his knife. "It's another one of those things you have to share to really enjoy."

Frances turned her head to look at him. "That's just what my mother used to say."

He chuckled. "Your mother sounds like my kind of woman!"

Frances had to concentrate not to roll her eyes. Mother was probably *exactly* his kind of woman—the kind who believed that a woman was incomplete without a husband, a home, and a litter. "I think she'd probably like you too," she mumbled. "Do you cook like this all the time?"

"Only for company. I'm just like you, I don't like cooking alone either."

"Company?" she queried.

His knife flashed over a spring carrot. "Franklin and Elaine come over occasionally, and Beth eats here a lot, particularly when we've had a long day. How are you coming with that?" He sidled down to peer over her shoulder, his head so close to hers that a strand of his hair brushed against her cheek. She tensed instantly, unaccustomed to having anyone so close. The knife slipped in her hand, missing her finger by only a breath.

"Hey—careful!"

She nodded, blushing a little, then brought the knife down for the last cut. "There," she said proudly, backing away from the pile of chopped celery, and away from him, "all finished. Anything else I can do?"

"Er—not really."

She glanced down the length of the counter and saw mound after mound of chopped vegetables and meat. She stared at it for a moment, then looked back at her own pathetically small pile, wonder how long he'd been waiting politely for her to finish. This was totally backward. Men weren't supposed to out-perform women in the kitchen.

"You did a wonderful job, though," said Ethan, as embarrassed to have done so much as she was to have done so little. "Just look at that!" he insisted, peering over her shoulder with a perfectly straight face. "Every piece is exactly the same size."

She rolled her head to meet his eyes, then they both stared at each other for a moment, mouths twitching, before bursting into simultaneous laughter.

They ate at the bar in the kitchen, perched on facing stools, oblivious to night's curtain coming down on the White Mountains outside the window. The pungent tang of pine wafted in through the screen to mingle with the aromas of ginger and garlic in the kitchen.

"This was absolutely fabulous," Frances sighed, putting down her fork at last, dabbing at the corners of her mouth with a napkin. She paused for effect, then added mischievously, "Especially the celery."

"Good Lord," he said, feigning shock. "You have a sense of humor!"

"I do not," she grinned. "You can ask anybody."

He set their plates off to one side, then rested his forearms on the bar between them and eyed her steadily. "What *would* they say, Frannie—the people in your life—if I asked about you? How would they describe you?"

She popped the last bite of a crusty roll into her mouth and considered the question, frowning. There weren't really many people in her life...except at work, of course. "Well...I suppose they would say I was good at my job."

He looked at her expectantly. "Go on."

Go on? What did he mean, go on? Trying to get ahead had consumed her life for the past eight years—there hadn't been time to get to know people, or to let them get to know her. Her co-workers were the only ones she ever came in contact with, and what else could they possibly say about her? That she was a good dresser?

Her mind scrambled for another answer, then her expression cleared. "They would say I was a woman in control of her life," she said proudly. "A woman on her way up; a woman making her mark on the world."

All of a sudden Ethan's eyes looked flat, like two silver-blue coins floating on the surface of his face. "What mark, Frannie?" he asked quietly.

Her brows twitched in confusion. "I've made a good life for myself." She could hear the petulance creeping into her voice. "And I'm proud of what I've accomplished, of how far I've come——" She clamped her mouth closed abruptly.

He was watching her carefully, his eyes in shadow so that she couldn't read them. "How far *have* you come, Frannie?"

Her mouth opened, closed, then opened again. "A long way," she whispered. "You have no idea how far."

"Then tell me."

Frances caught her lower lip between her teeth, then turned to look out at the shroud of darkness over the mountains, speckled now with a spattering of stars. She wanted to tell him. For some reason it was important that he knew.

She turned her head back to look at his shadowed face. The kitchen was almost fully dark now, and neither of them had thought to turn on a light, and somehow that seemed fitting.

"I never knew my father. He died before my first birthday," she began, looking down into her wine glass, speaking in a flat, unemotional monotone. "My mother raised me alone, in a part of the city people like you never see, in an apartment about the size of Elaine Harmon's kitchen." She hesitated, then condensed the years of watching her mother struggle into a single, understated phrase. "She deserved better than that, and I swore that one day, she'd have better—that we'd live in a fine house uptown, that we'd have nice things, that one day we'd rub elbows with the very people who were afraid to walk our street after dark."

He hadn't moved while she talked, but now he switched on the light over the bar so that she could see his expression. It seemed to reflect a knowledge of all the things she hadn't said, all the pain she'd glossed over. At some point—she hadn't noticed when—his hand had crossed the counter to hold hers. "Go on," he said.

She sighed heavily and shrugged. "There's nothing more to tell. I worked hard; I went to night school; I either fought the system or worked with it—whatever it took to get me where I wanted to go."

"And are you there now?"

She frowned at that, pressing her lips together. "I'm getting there."

"Then why aren't you happy?"

Her lips parted slightly as she heard the echo of her mother's voice, repeating again and again over the years, "I just wish you were happy, Frannie." What was the matter with these people? Bit by bit, day by day, she got closer to having everything she had ever wanted. Of course she was happy...except for this one little thing...

She pushed her fingers back through the mass of her hair, as if she were trying to push a nagging thought to the back of her brain, but it was hopeless. "I suppose it's funny, in a way," she said wryly. "All my plans, all that work, all those years struggling to get her out, and when I could finally do it, Mother wouldn't leave the old neighborhood. She's still there."

A trick of the light had softened the muscular squareness of his face, and he was smiling at her, as if she'd just solved a very complex problem. "Maybe she wasn't as anxious as you to leave so much behind."

Frances scowled and pressed her lips together, imagining for one startling moment that she could see her reflection in his eyes, and that that reflection wore pigtails and freckles and a hand-me-down dress with buttons that didn't match. "There was nothing there *to* leave behind."

His smile looked sad now. "Are you sure about that?"

She shook her head impatiently, trying to shake away the echo of her mother's voice telling her she couldn't leave the old neighborhood, that her life was there, and that some day Frannie would understand that.

Ethan was staring at her, so motionless that she wondered if he was even breathing. "You know how I know I'd like your mother, Frannie?" He didn't wait for an answer. "Because I see pieces of her whenever I look into your eyes. Sometimes—like when you're with that sick calf, or when you told Miles to call you Frannie—the woman you were meant to be shines through the woman you pretend to be, and that woman takes my breath away."

She was staring at him, forgetting to blink, her lips parted slightly. In some distant part of her mind, she was aware of him walking around the bar, taking both her hands in his and pulling her gently to her feet.

"Frannie," he murmured, his hands sliding up her arms to cradle her head, strong fingers deeply entwined in her hair. "She's in your eyes now, Frannie," he whispered. "The woman who takes my breath away."

Something in his eyes connected with something in hers, and the world seemed to stop for a moment, holding its breath, waiting for what would come next. Frances waited too, her breath caught in her throat, strangely powerless to initiate any action on her own. She could feel the heat emanating from his body, so close to hers that even a deep breath would bring them together, but she was incapable of even that much. Her own inability to act astounded her. Wasn't she the woman who was always in control? Where was all that control now?

The seconds stretched into an eternity of waiting while his head remained poised and hesitant mere inches from hers, and Frances trembled with heat from a dozen unexpected sources. She felt it course through her body like steaming liquid, simmering in the pit of her stomach and rising to expand within her breasts until they ached with the fire they contained. It was the very first time in her life that Frances had thought of her body as an instrument of pleasure, instead of merely as an instrument of work, and the thought made her smile, and the smile parted her lips, and the dance of love began.

He murmured something unintelligible as his lips touched hers, but the words were lost, and only the movement of his mouth had meaning. Because the last few seconds trailed behind her like empty years, wasted without his touch, the simple kiss became the climax of the almost unbearable tension, and rocked her with its impact. Somewhere deep within her, something wakened, blossomed, then flew upward through her body until it found expression in the tiny cry that escaped her lips. It traveled like a sigh from her mouth to his, inaudible to the world, but deafening to the man who received it.

Ethan pulled away quickly, stunned by the un-expected explosion of feeling that had traveled from her body to his. He was shaken like a young boy, only vaguely aware of his own ragged breathing, intensely conscious of the sudden need to possess her completely.

Frances tensed momentarily when his hands slid downward to press against her swollen breasts, but then he kissed her again and she felt herself wilting, dissolving as an entity, flowing inexorably toward him like an errant waterway tumbling toward the river it was destined to join. It was more than just a physical response; it was the essence of sharing, the willingness to commit oneself totally to another human being. Frances had never expected to feel such a thing. Later, it would occur to her that this was the moment she had fallen in love. For now, all she knew was that in some strange way Ethan belonged to her, and, more astounding still, she belonged to him.

The shrill jangle of the phone shattered the moment, broke the seal of their lips, and startled them both.

"Damn!" breathed Ethan, closing his eyes and resting his forehead against hers. "I have to answer that. It might be an emergency." He pulled away quickly, as if only a violent force could separate their bodies.

Frances simply stood there, dazed, the parts of her body that had been touching his suddenly, unbearably cold. Gradually the sound of his voice penetrated her consciousness.

"Take it easy, Leo—calm down. How bad is the bleeding? Can you get close to him...? Good. Just keep pressure on it. I'll be right there." He hung up quickly, turned to Frances with an apologetic look. "I'm sorry. There's been a trailering accident, and a horse has been cut up pretty badly. I have to go." His eyes pleaded for her to understand.

"Go," she said simply.

"Will you be here when I get back?"

Even with him standing on the other side of the room, her body could still feel the heat of his touch, her mind still reeled from the flood of awakened senses that had shattered her control—but fate had given her a chance to regain that control, and she had to take that chance. She shook her head. "I don't think so."

For just an instant, his blue eyes seemed to flicker with light, like a candle in the wind, then he sighed once and nodded. "It *will* happen, Frannie. You can't run away from something like this."

For the very first time, she was beginning to believe him.

It was barely midnight when Frances arrived back at the hotel, but the town was silent, and the street lamps painted their circles of light on empty pavements. She tiptoed into the lobby and closed the door quietly behind her, feeling a little like a kid trying to sneak in past curfew without waking her parents.

A rustle of paper from the sitting area on her left made her jump and catch her breath. Margaret was stretched out on a recliner, a magazine propped in her lap, dark, inquisitive eyes peering at Frances over a pair of reading glasses.

"I don't think I've ever seen you sitting down before, Margaret."

"Don't do much of it, as a rule." Margaret laid her magazine face down on the table next to her chair. "Did you have a nice evening?"

Frances hesitated for a beat. "Yes, yes, I did."

"Glad to hear it." Margaret eased herself up out of the recliner and started turning off the lamps one by one. "We'd both better get to bed. The heat's going to wake us early tomorrow. You see the ring around the moon tonight?"

Frances shook her head.

"Well, it's there; and that means we'll have humidity along with the heat. You'll be glad I made you buy that pair of shorts."

Frances nodded, walked to the stairs, climbed two steps, then turned and looked back at where Margaret was standing by the stairwell light switch, waiting to turn it off. "Have you ever been in love, Margaret?" she asked quietly.

Margaret didn't smile, exactly, but Frances had the feeling she wanted to. "Sure I was. Married too. Car accident killed him, almost twenty years ago now. This used to be our house." She did smile then, just a little. "Some day I'll tell you about him."

Some day. What a magical phrase that was, filled with unspoken promises. It made Frances smile. "I'd like that," she said, and she meant it.

CHAPTER EIGHT

THE sounds of morning drifted in through her hotel room window, waking Frances gently. She heard the bright chattering of birds greeting the sun, the strident crowing of a cock, muffled by distance, the rustle of tree leaves just outside her window. It was barely light, but already she could feel the promise of a blistering heat in the oppressive weight of the morning air.

Margaret had been right about the shorts, she thought with a smile.

She showered, washed her hair, then pulled it back into a ponytail to drip dry. She donned the white shorts and T-shirt with some reluctance, then decided to think of it as dressing for a tennis date. Somehow that made the brevity of the outfit acceptable.

Ethan was waiting in the hotel lobby when she came down for breakfast. He was slumped forward in a chair that faced the stairs, an elbow resting on each knee, his head hanging down between his shoulders. He was still wearing the black pants and white shirt he'd worn the night before, but there were circles of mud on his knees, and the shirt was stained and torn at the shoulder.

She stopped on the landing, one hand resting lightly on the banister. She heard the distant clatter of Margaret in the hotel kitchen, the sounds of the town stirring to life outside; but the lobby was an island of quiet.

"Good morning," she said, and his head lifted slowly. His face was drawn and pale beneath its tan; strands of sun-bleached blond lay over his forehead like someone's tangled knitting. There was an angry bruise high on his left cheekbone that made that eye seem a brighter shade of blue than the other. His gaze swept lazily from her face down to her bare legs, then back up to her eyes.

"You've got legs," he said, making an exausted attempt at a wolfish grin. "Great legs."

Frances pursed her lips in exasperation. "You look terrible. How did you get that bruise?"

He lifted one hand to touch his cheek gingerly. "The horse was bigger than I was."

"I hope he *looks* better than you do."

Ethan chuckled, then nodded. "He'll be fine."

"Good. Then you can go home and get some sleep..."

"Not a chance!"

She glared at him for a moment, hands on hips, then marched down the rest of the stairs toward him, a scold forming itself in her mind. She stopped abruptly, confused. She'd never scolded anyone in her whole life.

A twinkle lightened the weariness in his eyes and one side of his mouth curved upward lazily. "I belong right here, and you know it," he told her.

Her whole face seemed busy, brows twitching in confusion, her teeth kneading her lower lip.

His smile broadened. "We have to talk, Frannie."

She blinked at him, clasped her hands in front of her, then took a deep breath. "Oh?"

He eyed her steadily. "Something happened between us last night."

Color flooded her face and she looked down at her shoes.

"It isn't going to go away, Frannie."

Her brows furrowed hard. "Er—I was just going to have some breakfast..."

His eyes locked on hers. "Breakfast can wait."

"Good Lord, what happened to you?" Margaret stopped in the doorway, gaping at Ethan. Frances almost collapsed with relief at the interruption, but Ethan's eyes flickered with irritation.

"He's been on an emergency call all night, Margaret. I was just trying to talk him into having some breakfast..."

"You bet he'll have breakfast!" Margaret bustled over to grab Ethan's arm and pull him to his feet, her brow furrowed in concern. "Breakfast first, then a room. No way you're going to drive home before you get some sleep, Ethan Alexander!''

"I didn't come for breakfast, Margaret, and I don't need a room..."

"It's plain to see you're too tired to know what you need," she huffed. "Come on, Frannie. We'll all have breakfast in the kitchen..."

Margaret was a big, strong woman, but she looked almost petite when Ethan took her by the shoulders and held her still, looking down into her eyes. "Margaret," he said fondly, but firmly, "we can have breakfast later. Frannie and I need to talk first."

She sighed noisily, her big shoulders rising and falling with the effort. "Look at you!" she scolded. "You're hurt, you're tired, and you'd probably fall over if you weren't hanging on to me. Eat something, then sleep, then you can talk to your heart's content...tell him, Frannie." She glanced over her shoulder at Frances for support.

"She's right, Ethan..." Frances started to say, but his expression silenced her immediately.

"We *are* going to talk," he said in careful, measured tones, then he turned back to give Margaret a brief, tired smile. "Go on, now. We'll be along soon."

Margaret made an exasperated face and then left them alone.

Frances eyed Ethan warily, shifting her weight from one foot to the other like a tennis player waiting to receive a serve. He held her gaze without smiling, then gestured toward two wing chairs facing each other in the far corner of the room. "Let's sit down."

She sat on the edge of her chair, feet flat on the floor, hands folded tightly together in her lap, as nervous as she had ever been in her life. "Something happened between us last night," he'd said, and clearly that was what he wanted to talk about. She blushed furiously and looked down at her hands, hoping he didn't intend to rehash the events of the evening verbally. A gentleman would never do such a thing—but then who said Ethan Alexander was a gentleman?

When she risked a glance upward, Ethan was leaning forward in the chair that faced hers. His forearms were braced on his thighs, his hands were dangling between his knees, and his head was lifted to look straight at her. "Do you love your job, Frannie?" he asked suddenly.

She took a mental step backward. She wasn't sure what she'd expected him to say, but it certainly hadn't been that. "*That's* what you wanted to talk about? Whether or not I like my——"

"Well? Do you?"

"Of course I do." The answer was automatic, and maybe just a little too fast. "It's a good job. A great one, actually..."

"But do you *love* it?"

Frances leaned back in the chair and frowned at him from beneath lowered brows, retreating physically from the force of his questions.

"What's this all about? Why the sudden interest in my career?"

"I need to know how important it is to you."

"Why?"

He dropped his head and sighed. "Humor me, Frannie. Did you always want to be an insurance investigator? Did you dream about it when you were a little girl?"

"Of course not. I didn't even know what an insurance investigator was." She paused, studying his face carefully, looking for some dark motive behind the remarkable blue eyes. His expression was attentive, seemingly open, inviting her to continue. She shrugged and went on. "When I was old enough, I started looking for the kind of career that would give me what I wanted. Insurance seemed to be the answer. The schooling was relatively easy, the initial money was good, and the opportunities were almost limitless."

Ethan nodded once, eyes narrowed as he considered her answer. "So you don't really love your work; just what it can give you."

Frances stiffened defensively. "What's wrong with that?"

"Nothing, I suppose. Except that loving the end and not the means leaves a pretty big stretch of emptiness in between, doesn't it?"

Her lips tightened and she actually felt the yellow flash in her eyes. "Not all of us have the luxury of choosing a career we love," she said sharply.

"I know that, Frannie," he said gently. "The point I'm trying to make is that if you don't love your job you won't mind giving it up."

"Give it up?" she asked incredulously. "Why would I want to give it up?"

"So you could move up here, of course."

Her jaw dropped open.

"The way I see it," he went on blithely, "we're going to have to agree on where to live, or our marriage won't have much of a chance."

Frances felt the dry prickle of eyes held too wide, and had to concentrate to make herself blink.

"Not that I give it much of a chance anyway," Ethan chuckled, apparently oblivious to her astonishment. "We're total opposites. Look at you. Your values are all upside down, you're stubborn, defensive, materialistic . . . and, besides that, you dress funny."

Frances thought if her mouth fell open any further they'd be able to drive a truck through it.

"But be that as it may," Ethan went on, "marriage is all I've been thinking about since I saw you with the calf that first day."

Dumbfounded, she stared at him for an endless moment, her head shaking mindlessly. "This is the craziest conversation I've ever had in my life," she finally found her voice. "What are you talking about? Marriage? You and me? Are you out of your mind? We barely know each other.

Besides, I don't want to get married, I'm not sure I ever want to get married, and even if I did, I certainly wouldn't choose..." She stopped abruptly, uncomfortable with what she was about to say.

"A country vet who lives in Nowthen?" he finished her sentence with a lazy smile, but his eyes were fixed on hers with deadly seriousness. "It's a great place to raise kids, you know."

Frances tried to laugh, but it came out as a weak, breathy wheeze. She jumped when his hands reached across the space between them to grab hers.

"Don't you want kids, Frannie?"

"I...I never..."

"I was worried at first." He turned her hands over in his and looked down at her palms, studying them. "I was afraid you were all wrapped up in your career; that it was a calling, or something; that you wouldn't want to leave it behind." He pressed her palms together between his hands and looked up at her, smiling. "But that isn't going to be a problem, is it?"

She stared at him, mouth slightly open, eyes wide and unblinking. "You're crazy," she whispered, barely moving her lips.

He shrugged without taking his eyes from hers, still smiling, "Probably."

She nodded stupidly. "You got kicked in the head by a horse, and now you're crazy..."

He laughed out loud, then sobered a little. "Crazy to want to marry you, or crazy to think you'd want to marry me...which is it?"

"Both."

His smile blossomed again, but he released her hands and eased back in the chair. The bruise on his cheek seemed darker now, and there were faint white lines of exhaustion around his mouth.

He's tired, Frances thought, maybe even delirious, and he just doesn't know what he's saying. "You need to get some rest," she started to say, but then Margaret appeared in the doorway, her hands punched into the rolls at her waist, a scowl firmly in place.

"Breakfast," she growled, glaring at Ethan. "Now!"

While Margaret served bacon, eggs, coffee and orange juice, Ethan and Frannie eyed each other across the table. His gaze warned that their conversation wasn't over—only temporarily interrupted—but by the time he'd finished eating his eyelids drooped heavily, and Frances had a reprieve.

"Are you ready to admit you need a room now?" chided Margaret, eyeing his slumped posture.

He lifted his head and smiled weakly. "Maybe that's not such a bad idea. But you and I," his gaze rolled toward Frances, "have some unfinished business to take care of later."

Frances looked embarrassed, while Margaret looked at one, then the other, her eyes bright with curiosity. There was an uncomfortable silence around the table for a moment.

"Come on, Ethan," Margaret said at last, pushing herself to her feet, her broad hands braced on the table. "I'll open a room for you."

He rose slowly from his chair, his eyes still fixed on Frances. "Don't run away, Frannie," he said softly, smiling.

Frances sat immobile for what seemed like a long time after they'd left, staring at her folded hands. When she heard the tread of footsteps on the floor above she awakened from what seemed like a brief, mindless sleep, looked around, and saw the back door. She rose slowly, walked stiffly toward the door, then left the hotel.

The heat was already oppressive, the air thick and difficult to breathe, but Frances kept walking, as if physical motion would somehow relieve the muddle of her thoughts.

Don't run away, he'd said—it seemed he was always saying that; probably because you're always running away, she thought wryly. But you're not going to do that this time. After all, what's to run from? A half-baked marriage proposal from a man who could barely keep his eyes open? He'd probably never remember half of what he had said anyway. And so what if she'd found herself surrendering to the skillful seduction of an attractive man...what was so frightening about that? It happened to millions of women every day. Just because it had never happened to her before didn't necessarily mean she was immune...

You always have been before, a little voice reminded her, but she ignored it.

Besides, physical attraction was simply that; a fleeting, purely biological function that didn't have to change the way you lived or the way you thought or the values you held...

Unless those had never really been your values, a little voice persisted...

"Frannie! Hi!"

Startled, she turned to see a vaguely familiar face smiling at her from across the village green. She lifted a hand tentatively and waved, received a vigorous wave in response, then recognized the merry features of the woman who had waited on her when Margaret had taken her clothes shopping.

"How's Ethan?" the woman called out. Frances couldn't remember her name; couldn't imagine why the woman would ask *her* how Ethan was.

"Fine," she called back, her voice uncertain.

"Well, tell him we'll see him tonight, when he comes back to check on Leo's stallion again." Frances's face cleared in sudden understanding. "Sorry we ruined your evening last night."

The smile froze on her face as she wondered what Ethan had told them about "their evening."

She walked on down the main street, her thoughts busy, her eyes fixed on the pebbled concrete walk receding beneath the round toes of her tennis shoes. She caught herself overstepping the cracks in the walk, just as she had as a child.

Someone rapped on a store window as she passed, and waved to her when she looked—another vaguely familiar face...perhaps someone she'd met in the park with Elaine that night? She returned the wave with a smiling shrug and walked on.

It was a nice town, she decided, slowing her pace, looking around as she strolled. Elderly trees shaded the main street, draping lacy arms over shopfront benches. Later in the morning, neighbors would probably sit on those benches and pass the time of day, trading those little bits of information that, over the years, nurture a lasting friendship.

It wouldn't be so bad, she thought, living in a place like this, forever surrounded by friends so close that they became family...and almost as soon as the thought had formed in her mind she stopped dead on the walk. What was she thinking of? Was she actually taking all that talk about marriage seriously?

"Well, Frannie, you're up and about early."

Frances jumped and turned at the sound of Elaine's voice behind her.

"Good heavens, child, you're jumpy as a rabbit! I didn't mean to scare you."

"You just startled me a little," Frances smiled wanly. "How's Franklin?"

"Better. Frustrated, though, not being able to use his hands."

"And the calf?"

"You and that calf!" Elaine smiled, shaking her head. "You sure got attached to each other in a hurry, didn't you?"

Frances felt her smile falter. It wasn't really that she was *attached* to the calf; she just thought about it every now and then, that was all. People didn't get attached to animals; not normal people...

"...so I think Ethan may want to take a look at her today," Elaine was saying, and Frances snapped back to attention.

"Why?" she asked quickly. "What's wrong with her?"

Elaine frowned and cocked her head, puzzled. "I just told you, dear. Beth says her temperature's up a bit. Nothing to panic about, but you can't be too careful with burns, you know. How was your dinner last night, by the way?" She was smiling again, her dark eyes glinting with mischief.

Frances sighed, exasperated. "Does *everybody* in this town know I went to Ethan's last night?"

Elaine chuckled. "Not yet. But then again, it's early." Her cheeks dimpled with her smile. "I'd better be getting home. We have a late calf due today, and Franklin may need some help. Come out and see us, Frannie.''

"I will," she promised. "Just as soon as I have the claim forms for you to sign.''

"You don't need an excuse to visit friends, you know.'' Elaine squeezed Frances's hand. "Don't forget to tell Ethan about the calf,'' she called over her shoulder as she walked away.

Frances continued to wander past the rest of the main street shops. In the next hour she ran into half a dozen other people who greeted her by name, even though she couldn't remember meeting them all. The overt friendliness of strangers should have been unsettling—it certainly would have been on the busy streets of downtown Boston—but somehow it wasn't. She found herself responding to each new greeting with a smile that became more natural as the morning wore on, and it occurred to her that an onlooker might think she actually belonged in this town. Lord knew, she was dressed for the part!

The thought made her stop and frown down at her legs, already turning pink from the unaccustomed time in the sun, and she decided to return to the hotel. She spent the rest of the morning at the desk in her room, working on the Harmon claim, trying to track down Nowthen's volunteer firemen by phone. Four of the men were "out in the fields cultivating corn," whatever that meant, and the fifth was visiting relatives in Florida. Her pen rested over the blank space that usually summarized an arson squad report. What was she supposed to write? Reports unavailable due to corn?

She puzzled over that, ankles wrapped around the legs of her chair, twirling a strand from her ponytail around one finger. "Come in," she answered a rap on the door absently.

She felt a draught from the hall as the door opened, and then, "Hi, Frannie."

Her lips lifted automatically at the sound of that voice, as if every minute of the morning had been spent just waiting to hear it again. She turned her head slowly, unaware that her expression had softened, that her eyes were shining like polished chips of amber. "Hello, Ethan." She loved saying his name. Had she said it before? She couldn't remember.

He was framed in the doorway, legs spread, hands thrust into his pant pockets. The sunlight from the window wove golden threads through his sleep-tousled hair. "I'm going home to shower and change," he said. "I want you to come with me."

Frances felt a deep, perfect silence settle over the room as she looked at him. What passed from his eyes to hers in that silence made pretence foolish. "I don't think that would be a very good idea," she whispered.

"Yes, you do."

She felt something deep inside slipping away, something she thought might have been important once, but she couldn't quite remember what that something was, or why she should care about it.

"You don't understand," she said. Her voice sounded strangely distant, somehow muted. "I'm not good at...casual relationships."

"There's nothing casual between us, Frannie. I thought that was pretty clear after our talk this morning."

She frowned hard and caught her lower lip between her teeth. "I don't understand what's happening," she whispered, the words coming out in a soft, breathless rush of confusion.

"Yes, you do," Ethan said for the second time in as many minutes. He took a step away from the door, closing it behind him with a casual flip of his fingers. The click of the latch engaging sounded like a distant gunshot.

Frances sat motionless in the chair as he crossed the room, his eyes never leaving hers, and when he stopped next to her she realized she should jump up and run; that she should have run for her life the first time she ever saw this man, because her life was precisely what he threatened. If she let him touch her again; if she let herself sink any deeper into the blue depths of his eyes, Frances Hudson of the designer suits, the luxurious town house, the expensive car and the enviable career—that Frances Hudson would simply cease to exist. She would disappear under his touch as if she had never been, and in her place would be...

"Frannie," he murmured as his hands came down on her shoulders. "My beautiful Frannie..."

It seemed so strange that just a moment before she had been frozen in her chair, her ankles wound around its legs so tightly that her skin would bear the marks for hours—and yet he pulled her effortlessly to her feet, effortlessly against him, as if that was where her body had always wanted to be.

Mesmerized, hypnotized, she looked up at him as his hands moved to cradle her head, as his eyes traveled her face in a blue, searing journey of possession. His mouth followed the path his eyes had taken, brushing at her forehead, her eyelids, her cheeks, finally finding the soft, swollen centre of her upper lip. Softly, delicately, he tasted, pulled away, then came back again and again until Frances felt her breath coming in short, soft gasps.

"Frannie," he breathed her name against her mouth, into her mouth, filling her up with the sound and the feel of who she was meant to be, who she *was* at this moment.

Somehow her hands had become trapped between them, and she pressed against the wall of his chest, protesting breathlessly, "This is too soon, too fast—it's all happening too fast..."

"How long does it take, Frannie? How long does it take to see what you want, what you've always wanted, and reach out and make it yours?"

She had no time to reply, no time to even think of a reply, because in the next instant his mouth claimed hers with a frantic pressure that was almost bruising. There was a flutter of air as his hands pulled her T-shirt from her shorts, then slipped beneath it to splay against the bare skin of her back. She felt the hard ridges of his callused fingers scrape downward to clutch at her waist, then jerk her hard against him. Somehow her hands found the solid contours of his biceps, and then without conscious direction, reached up to grasp the back of his head. The motion lifted her swollen breasts against his chest, making him tense and gasp aloud.

"You . . . were . . . going home," she reminded him, struggling for enough breath to speak.

"I am home," he replied hoarsely, sweeping her off the floor and against his chest with a single fluid gesture. "We both are," he murmured into her neck, then he carried her to the bed.

Frances lay on the patterned quilt looking up into the iridescent blue of his eyes. She watched her fingers threading through the sun-bleached strands of his hair, wondering how her hands had learned to do such a thing. There had been no time in her life for men or relationships—certainly not love, or what a young woman might mistake for love—and yet her body responded to this man with the ease born of experience she had never had.

When he removed his shirt her hands traced the contours of muscular shoulders, arms, chest, as if she had done it a hundred times before. When his hands slipped beneath the front of her T-shirt to explore the heated mounds of flesh beneath, the shivering thrill was oddly familiar, as if her body had always contained the knowledge her mind had denied, as if she'd known everything about lovemaking all along.

As his hands and mouth continued the ritual of love, her back arched, her breath caught in her throat, and she realised she hadn't known everything after all.

Sunlight dappled the quilted spread beneath their glistening bodies, then moved with the clock to paint circles of light higher on the wall. From her nest within Ethan's arms, Frances watched the journey of the light without any awareness of the passage of time it represented. Time was part of the old world, the world that existed outside this room, and she didn't want it to intrude. When the phone rang, she burrowed her face deeper into his chest and closed her eyes. His muscles elongated beneath her as he reached for the phone, then she felt the vibrations of his voice rumbling in his chest.

"I have to go, Frannie," he murmured tenderly as he replaced the receiver, one arm still holding her close. "That was Elaine."

Frances tensed and looked up at him, her eyes panicked. "But I just talked to her a little while ago, and she said the calf had a temperature, but she didn't think it was serious, she just said to tell you to come out when you woke up..."

"Relax!" he smiled at her reaction. "It isn't your calf. One of the cows needs a little help calving, that's all." He smiled, those bluer than blue eyes dazzling her, commanding the response he wanted without the necessity of words.

"I'm coming with you," she said, feeling very much like the pigtailed Frannie who wanted to tag along, and, at the same time, very much like a full-grown woman compelled to follow a particular man wherever he chose to lead. Oddly enough, those two personalities seemed suddenly inseparable.

CHAPTER NINE

A HOT, sultry wind whipped through the open windows of the truck as Frances and Ethan sped toward the Harmon farm. The silence between them seemed to crackle with the energy of words not yet spoken, sharpening senses and magnifying the impact of every stimulus.

Frances felt the wind against her face like the press of a giant hand, felt the dampened shirt cling to her skin like a lover's caress. When a bead of sweat trickled down the valley between her breasts she shivered and plucked the shirt away from her body.

Ethan glanced over at the motion. "Should I turn on the air conditioner?"

She shook her head quickly. If he turned on the air conditioner, they'd have to close the windows, and then the blurred kaleidoscope of color wouldn't be so brilliant; the pungent, earthy odors of the country would be locked outside, and the physical discomfort that was reminding her she was alive would be gone. It never occurred to her that these were things she would have struggled to avoid just a few days ago.

He nodded. "We're almost there anyway."

It was only when the truck pulled into the Harmon drive that her thoughts faltered. Back at the hotel, she had never really considered where Ethan was going or what would happen there; only that she wanted to be with him. But now, as they rounded the house and pulled up in front of the calving barn, the bawling of an animal in pain brought home the reality of the situation. What was she doing here?

She froze in the seat as he brought the truck to a stop and turned off the engine.

"Have you ever seen anything born, Frannie?" he asked, and she marveled at the nonchalance in his voice. Her ponytail whipped back and forth as she shook her head. She jumped when his hand touched her arm. The cow was bawling louder now, and she winced at the sound.

"You don't have to come in, you know," he said gently. "But it sounds worse than it is. Elaine said it's a clean breech; once I turn the calf, the birth should be easy."

Frances grimaced. "Maybe I'll just wait here——"

Suddenly Beth's slight figure emerged from the calving barn and she hurried over to Ethan's side of the truck. "Hi, you two!" she called.

"What's the situation?" asked Ethan.

"It's a clean breech, just like Elaine said; it's the burned calf I'm worried about."

Frances stiffened and leaned across the seat. "What's the matter with her?" she asked.

Beth frowned and lifted one shoulder. "She seemed fine when I left last night, but she hasn't eaten since, and she's running a low-grade temp." She met Ethan's eyes directly, communicating something Frances didn't understand.

"Listless?" he asked quietly, and Beth nodded with a grim expression that made Frances's stomach tighten.

"What does it mean if she's listless?" she asked in a whisper, almost afraid to hear the answer.

The bawling from the calving barn interrupted before he could speak, and Ethan jumped quickly out of the truck. "I've got to get in there, Frannie," he called over his shoulder as he and Beth sprinted away. For a moment Frances sat in the truck, perfectly still, wincing at every pained call from the laboring cow. After a short time the noise from the calving barn ceased, and the only sound was the wind rustling through the new corn, the rasp of grasshoppers feasting in the back field. There was no sound at all from the little white building where the burned calf was kept. Slowly, fearfully, Frances got out of the truck, crossed the yard, and entered the black doorway.

"Hey, girl," she whispered, pausing until her eyes adjusted to the gloom, then making her way down the aisle to the calf's stall. She breathed a sigh of relief to find the calf lying comfortably on its stomach with its front legs tucked around its chest. The bony head turned slowly as she entered the stall, and large, moist brown eyes greeted her with a blink. Frances chuckled nervously, and the calf bleated once.

"Well, baby, there's nothing wrong with you, is there?" she crooned, squatting on her heels and reaching out to stroke the calf's neck. "You're not listless, are you? You're just sleepy, and that's okay. You're just a baby, after all, and babies are always sleepy."

The calf's eyelids drooped languorously as she continued to caress it.

"That's right, go to sleep, baby," she murmured, moving her hand down the broad forehead between the soulful eyes, farther down to the wide black nose. The calf grunted softly, then swiped once at her palm with its tongue before dropping its head to rest on its forelegs. "That's a girl," Frances crooned, settling down to sit on the mats at the calf's side, continuing her mindless caressing as the calf's eyes fell closed. "You sleep now. You rest."

She didn't know how long she sat there, stroking the tiny creature, absently humming a lullaby she remembered from her childhood; but suddenly she felt an emptiness, a sense of aloneness that hadn't been there a moment before. Her hand stilled on the calf's neck, her eyes widened, and she held her breath.

Silence. Complete and awful silence.

She stared down at the calf, afraid to blink, afraid that in that instant of sightlessness she would miss what she wanted to see.

Breathe—her mind whispered the word as her gaze remained riveted to the calf's motionless ribcage. Breathe—her mind repeated the command over and over, until her lips finally gave voice and she said it aloud, but the little body remained still.

She frowned hard at the ugly creature with its patchwork of healing burns and straggly hair, thinking she would give anything she owned, anything she treasured, just to see those liquid eyes open again—not because this animal had been a huge part of her life, but just because the world was a little emptier now, with one less heartbeat in it.

Ethan found her sitting next to the calf, her white shorts blackened by the mats on the stall floor, her hand resting lightly on the lifeless neck. He stopped in the stall doorway, stared at the calf for a long moment, then looked at her, his expression pained.

"Frannie?" he whispered, and she turned empty eyes to look up at him. He was moving across the stall to take her in his arms, to give comfort, when she spoke.

"She's dead!"

Ethan stopped, flinching at the tone of accusation. His brows twitched and his chest lifted with a deep breath. "We did everything we could for her, Frannie."

"Obviously it wasn't enough," she mumbled bitterly, turning back to look at the calf, biting down hard on her lower lip.

Ethan was silent for a moment, then he spoke carefully. "Life ends, Frannie. No matter how much we want it to go on, no matter how long we try to prolong it, when it's time, life just ends."

Her lips quivered as she fought to hold back the tears. "It's not fair! She was just a baby."

Ethan approached her cautiously, almost as if he expected her to dart away. She lifted her head at the gentle pressure of his hand on her shoulder. "Come on, Frannie," he said, holding out his hand and helping her to her feet.

She allowed herself to be led out of the little white building that had become a tomb, across the sun-baked barnyard, through the wide doorway of the calving barn. She was barely aware of Elaine and Franklin leaning over the metal bars of a large stall, of Beth standing knee-deep in bloodied straw, beaming down at a slick fawn-colored bundle. She raised her head and grinned at Frances. "Isn't she beautiful?"

Frances glanced coldly at the new calf. She wasn't so beautiful. She was wet and scrawny and mindless, her head wobbling on a weak neck as she responded to the vigorous lash of her mother's tongue.

"The burned calf died," Ethan said quietly from behind her.

"Oh, Frannie, I'm sorry!" Elaine put in quickly. "I know how attached you were to her."

Frances looked at her. "I wasn't attached to her," she protested quickly. "It's just that...I never saw anything die before..." She shrugged and her voice faded away as she looked back at the new calf.

There was a long silence and then Franklin leaned heavily against the bars, his bandaged hands dangling down into the stall as he stared at his new calf. "Funny how things balance, isn't it?" he asked no one in particular. "One dies, another's born."

Frances looked over at him, appalled that these people could be so accepting; that they weren't as devastated by the calf's death as she was.

Her eyes searched Franklin's weathered, seamed face, then Elaine's kind, maternal countenance, then Beth's, and, finally, Ethan's. In each she saw a measure of sadness, but beneath that was the serenity of resignation.

Was that what you learned, living in a place like this? she wondered. That you accepted things as they were without a single word or gesture of protest? If she had lived *her* life that way, she'd still be in a second-floor tenement with nothing to show for the years behind her, no hope for a better future...

"I can't stay here," she whispered suddenly, her eyes focused on Ethan with the bright panic of a trapped animal. "I'm...sorry..."

"It's all right, Frannie, I understand."

Her mouth twitched in a weak, helpless smile, because he didn't understand—not really. None of them did.

He pressed the truck keys into her hand and said something about getting a ride into town with Beth later, but Frances barely heard him. Ethan and Elaine followed as far as the barn doorway, and stood there watching as Frances crossed the yard and climbed into the truck.

"She's taking it hard, Ethan," Elaine murmured, her brows puckered in a worried frown.

"I know. I was afraid she might."

"Maybe you should go with her."

His eyes narrowed as he watched the truck disappear in a cloud of dust. "She needs time, Elaine; time to come to terms with death on her own. Otherwise she'll never understand what's really important in life."

Elaine slipped her arm through his and squeezed fondly. "You're hopelessly in love with her, aren't you?"

He closed his eyes and the words escaped in a soft, sharp exhalation. "Oh, yes."

"Don't let her get away."

He stared at the place in the drive he had seen the truck last, the peacock blue of his eyes bright with determination. "I won't," he whispered. "Not if I can help it."

Frances parked Ethan's truck at an angle to the curb and started up the hotel's front walk. She moved like an old woman, eyes cast downward, shoulders slumped.

Margaret looked up from polishing the window in the front door, wiped a heavy forearm across her brow, then rolled her eyes. "I see you've ruined another outfit," she scolded good-naturedly.

Frances paused on the steps up to the porch to glance at the dust smears on her once-white T-shirt and shorts, the tiny calf hairs that still clung where she had wiped her hand. Her mouth twitched and she looked up at Margaret. The wind had freed strands of her hair from her ponytail, and they lay across her face like streaks of caramel; there were dusty smudges where she'd pushed it off her forehead; but it was the expression in her eyes that gave Margaret pause. The yellow spark of life that usually flashed from those light brown circles was gone, and they looked flat, empty.

"What's wrong?" Margaret asked, instantly alert. "Where's Ethan?"

"Nothing's wrong," Frances said tiredly. "Ethan is still at the Harmons', taking care of a new calf. He'll be by for the truck later."

Margaret nodded silently, her head tipped to one side. "You sure you're okay?"

Frances forced a smile. "I'm fine, Margaret. Just tired." She moved woodenly across the porch, through the front door, and climbed the stairs inside to her room. She stopped just inside the door, staring at the tousled covers, then closing her eyes at the memory they evoked. It seemed as if a million years had passed since she'd been in that bed with Ethan, rosy with the afterglow of love, thinking that life couldn't possibly exist outside the circle of his arms.

It was really true, she thought cynically; all the things they said about love being blind and passion robbing you of reason—it was all true.

She'd wanted Ethan—wanted him so badly that she'd fooled herself into believing she could actually live in his world; that maybe his world was even better than hers. But it wasn't. His world was filled with blood and bruises and illness and death and placid people who lay down and let the vagaries of fate roll right over them. She didn't belong here.

The phone jangled on the nightstand, making her jump.

"Frances? Is that you?"

She took a breath and straightened, as if the president of Northeastern Casualty could actually see her through the phone. "Yes, sir, this is Frances."

"You sound a little strange...everything all right up there?"

"Yes, sir, everything's fine. Did you receive my preliminary report?"

"I've got it right here, Frances. That's why I'm calling. Seems pretty clear that the Harmons have a legitimate claim, so there's no point in dragging out the investigation. Why don't you come on back to the city? I'll bet you've had enough of farm country to last you a lifetime."

Because he seemed to be waiting for a comment, Frances said, "It certainly isn't Boston, sir."

He laughed heartily. "No, I'll just bet it isn't! You tie up whatever loose ends you have there, then come home and recuperate for a week or so. After that, I've got an assignment you're going to love. Our Paris office requested some help with an investigation over there, and I promised I'd send the best man I had. As it happens, the best man I have happens to be a woman." There was silence on the line for a moment. "You, Frances," he prompted. "You're the best investigator we've got, and it's time you knew it."

"Oh!" It was more an exclamation of surprise than a word, and it elicited a chuckle.

"It's not just empty praise, Frances. You'll find a healthy salary increase in your next check."

Frances swallowed and blinked. "I don't know what to say..."

"Don't say anything. Just pack up and get back here. On top of all the work waiting for you, the Kirov Ballet opens in three days, and I know you don't want to miss that."

"No," Frances said, her lips strangely numb, "I certainly don't."

She sank to the bed after hanging up the phone and just sat there, mindlessly stroking the bright squares of the quilt, staring off into the distance.

She'd made it. She'd finally made it to where she'd always wanted to be. Top investigator; salary increase; nights at the ballet and trips to Europe...*that* was her life; *that* was what she'd been working for all these years. *That* was where she belonged.

A faint smile crossed her lips as she continued to sit and stare, imagining the wonders of what waited for her in Boston, her hand still absently stroking the quilt beneath her, smoothing out all the wrinkles lovemaking had left behind.

CHAPTER TEN

FRANCES bent over the suitcase on the bed, folding the last silk blouse into place. She was dressed in a conservative navy suit with crisp white piping, and once again her hot caramel hair was tamed and trapped in a coil at the base of her neck. Solid gold buttons winked expensively in her ears. She jumped at the sudden loud banging on her door, then jerked her head when it flew open and crashed against the wall.

"Ethan!" she whispered, staring at the figure that seemed to fill the doorway, his broad shoulders nearly touching the frame on either side, his blond hair brushing the underside of the lintel. She had prepared herself mentally for seeing him one last time before she left town; steeled herself for the effect his presence always had on her; but all the preparation in the world couldn't keep her heart from turning over at the sight of him.

In the space of an instant she saw and memorized a score of things: the tanned, muscular forearms beneath the rolled-up sleeves of a fresh denim shirt; the ripple of thigh muscles under jeans faded by countless washings; the angry, purplish bruise high on his left cheek, giving his face a sinister cast. His newly washed hair fell over his brow in a boyish tumble; a strangely innocent touch that seemed terribly out of place against the angry blue sparks of his eyes. "What the hell do you think you're doing?" he growled.

She hesitated for a moment, intimidated by the low rumble of his voice, and it occurred to her then that she had never heard him speak in anger. She straightened to her full height and took a deep breath. "I'm packing," she said with forced calm, her light brown eyes never wavering from his.

"I can see that!" he shouted, wincing immediately at the volume of his own voice. He sighed heavily, then stepped into the room and pushed the door shut behind him. "Margaret said you'd settled your bill, but I couldn't believe you'd leave without——"

"I wouldn't," she interrupted quietly. "I would have found you first. I wouldn't leave without saying goodbye."

His shoulders moved in a silent, humorless laugh, then he cocked his head and stared at her, eyes traveling the full length of her body in slow disbelief. "Good Lord, Frannie, what the hell are you doing? What the hell have you *done*? Look at yourself!" He scowled at her hair, her clothes. "You look like——"

"I look like myself," she said firmly, turning back to her packing. "Frances Hudson. That's who I am, you know." She closed the lid of the suitcase, snapped the latch, then let her fingers rest on the smooth leather for a moment. The bright colors of the quilt beneath the case caught her eye, mocking her with the poignant memories of the things she had felt on that quilt just a few hours before. She closed her eyes and fought to keep the memories at bay. "Ethan," she spoke without looking up, "I don't belong here. I never did. And I can't stay."

In the deep silence that followed, Frances imagined she could hear the beating of two hearts in the room, just slightly out of sync. She was afraid to look up, not just because she was afraid to see anger or disappointment or disbelief in his face, but simply because she was afraid to see his face at all. Whatever the expression, he would look at her with those eyes—those damnable blue eyes that seemed to touch her in a place she'd never been touched before—and she would weaken. She would do anything he said, anything he asked, even if it was the wrong thing for both of them. She needed another heartbeat, another breath, another moment to gather her strength before she could look at those eyes again.

"Frannie——"

"Don't call me that!"

She heard the sound of air passing through his lips.

"You *do* belong here, Frannie. You belong here with me."

She pressed her lips into a tight, bloodless line and shook her head. "I almost started to believe that...almost...but I was wrong."

"Then what the hell happened here?" he demanded furiously, his voice so powerful that Frances felt like a swimmer struggling to stay erect under the force of a mighty wave. "Explain to me what happened right in this room just a few hours ago! Dammit, Frannie, *talk* to me! Look at me!" He crossed the room in two strides, grabbed her by the arm, then spun her to face him. The suddenness of the gesture loosened one of the pins holding her hair, and it fell to the wooden floor with a tiny clatter. To Frances, it sounded like a piece of herself being shaken from its moorings; as if he was trying to destroy the person she was to make room for the person he wanted her to be.

She raised her eyes to meet his at last. "What happened in this room was a mistake," she said tremulously. "What happened in this *town* was a mistake. You all treated me like...like... someone else, and, after a while, I almost *became* that someone else." She closed her eyes briefly and licked her lips. "I almost forgot who I was," she ended in a whisper.

Something shifted behind his eyes, making them seem darker. "We treated you like the person you are," he said darkly, "not like the person you pretend to be."

"This *is* the person I am," she insisted, spreading her arms as if presenting herself for inspection. "I'm Frances Hudson. I live in Boston. I have an excellent career, a bright future, a beautiful home and..."

He'd folded his arms across his chest and was just standing there, listening patiently, and something about that seemed to diminish the accomplishments she was itemizing.

"Oh, never mind!" She flapped her hand at him and scowled. "You wouldn't understand."

"I understand perfectly. You grew up poor, envying the rich, so you worked your whole life to get to where you thought they were, and now you count your blessings in *things*." Ethan smiled coldly at her expression. "You see, Frances? I *do* understand."

She tried to stare him down, but for some reason she felt an inexplicable urge to simply burst into tears.

"The calf did it, didn't she?" he asked sharply. "It was that damn calf dying..."

"The calf..." Her voice cracked and she had to pause to swallow before she could go on. "The calf snapped me out of a silly fantasy, that's all!" she shouted, her voice quavering dangerously.

"You couldn't stand losing it," he hammered her with his words. "She was the first thing in your life that really mattered, and you can't deal with losing important things, can you, Frannie? So you don't *collect* important things, you just fill your life with what you can stand to loose, like beautiful homes and big cars and——''

"That's not true!" she shouted, fists clenched at her sides, her body so rigid that the muscles in her neck ached.

He looked at her for a long time, and gradually his expression softened, and one corner of that beautiful, chiseled mouth turned up in a sad smile. In an unbelievably tender, cherishing gesture, he reached out and cradled her chin in the cup of his fingers. "You'll never find in Boston what you could have here with me, Frannie. Money can't buy it. And the sad thing is that the real woman hiding beneath that silly suit never really wanted to be rich . . . you just didn't want to be poor. Somewhere along the way you've forgotten the difference."

"That doesn't make sense," she whispered, unreasonably paralyzed simply because his fingers still cupped her chin, unreasonably disappointed when he finally let his hand drop.

"Yes, it does," he sighed, hunching his shoulders, shoving his hands into the front pockets of his jeans. "It makes perfect sense." He looked down at the floor for a moment, and the moment stretched endlessly as Frances looked at the shadows crossing his strong face, softening the clarity of his features.

He raised his head and smiled at her—a strange, heartbreakingly beautiful smile beneath eyes filled with inexpressible sadness. "If you

ever see Frannie again," he said softly, "tell her
I love her." Then he shrugged and turned for the
door.

Frances just stood there mute, blinking after
him.

The drive back to Boston seemed interminable.
For the first hour and a half the highway wound
endlessly through wooded hills and empty
countryside, as if the rest of civilization had
somehow disappeared while she was in Nowthen.
The road seemed deserted in these sparsely settled
areas, and with only an occasional car or truck
to distract her, France began to feel as though
she were doomed to travel forever on a highway
that went nowhere.

Only a little farther and the signs of civilization will begin again, she kept telling herself.
Just a little farther and I'll start to see billboards
and housing developments and the pall of city
pollution sitting on the horizon . . . but the silent
woods and the empty fields kept marching by,
and eventually her thoughts turned to self-
recrimination.

I should have at least called the Harmons to
say goodbye, she chastized herself; and I should
have tried to explain things to Margaret so she
wouldn't have looked at me that way when I
walked out . . .

She winced even now, remembering the expression on Margaret's face. "I don't under-

stand," the older woman had mumbled gruffly, her hands worrying her apron. "Why are you leaving so fast? Are you coming back? What about Ethan?" Frances hadn't trusted herself to speak then; she'd only been able to shake her head, over and over again.

Now, with the security of Boston so far in the distance that she began to feel she would never arrive, she began to look back on the time she had spent in Nowthen with an almost painful longing.

She'd felt safe there, she realized suddenly; not just safe from the hazards of city life, but emotionally safe—as if the people of Nowthen had woven a caring emotional buffer around their little corner of the world that protected everyone in it.

Her lips moved against one another as she remembered the band concert in the park and the unexpected sense of community she'd felt there: Elaine's warmth, Miles's giving her his handkerchief to wipe the ice cream from her hands, Ethan next to her on the bench with the setting sun dancing in his hair...

And then she thought of gruff, taciturn Margaret taking her to buy clothes; strangers greeting her on the street as if she were one of them; Ethan giving a stray dog her name...

She didn't want to think of him specifically, but he kept creeping into every thought, like a common thread weaving the fabric of her memories of Nowthen together.

"Ethan," she whispered his name aloud in the luxurious quiet of her car, and the sound shattered the dam holding back the most intense of her feelings. For a moment she thought she might drown in the flood.

Even with every minute increasing the miles between them, freeze-frame images of him lingered in her mind's eye with stunning clarity—Ethan standing in the aisle of the calf barn that first day, his smile radiating light; Ethan rushing into his office, dripping wet from the shower and clutching a towel around his waist, soothing the frantic dog he'd given her name; Ethan slumped in the chair in the hotel lobby waiting for her, his face lined with weariness and marked with the bruise left by Leo's injured stallion; Ethan braced over her on the bed . . . she caught her breath, re-living that moment, imagining she could actually feel the weight of his body, the hot, sweet press of his mouth against hers, the prickly rasp of his unshaven jaw on the soft flesh of her breast . . .

She squeezed her eyes shut briefly, fighting the merciless, suffocating onslaught of memory, her hands locked desperately around the wheel as if it were her only lifeline.

You could have all that again, Frances, a little voice whispered in the back of her mind. All you have to do is go back; just turn the car around and go back; back to Nowthen, back to Ethan. He said you were running, and you are. But what are you running from?

Frances couldn't remember. She blinked at the highway rolling steadily upward under the wheels of her car, her thoughts numb, barely aware that she was watching for a place to turn and go back.

Suddenly she reached the summit of the hill she'd been climbing and a large green and white sign loomed just ahead. "Boston—35 miles" it read, and, as her eyes scoured the distance, she could see the fringes of the world she had always known shimmering on the horizon below. As the car plunged downward the beginnings of civilization began to unroll past the car like a red carpet of welcome—scattered hobby farms at first, then housing developments, then the clusters of commercial businesses and restaurants displacing the forests. Now she could see the blurred spires of Boston pointing skyward like fingers sprouting from the hand of the earth. She sped past exit after exit, her eyes fixed on the distant city, forgetting that just a few moments before she'd been thinking of turning around and going back to Nowthen. Her home lay directly ahead; the only home she had ever known.

It was full dark by the time Frances turned the key in her town house door. Physically and emotionally exhausted, she stepped into the foyer, switched on the lights, and waited for the warm feeling of home envelop her. She stood quietly for a moment, still waiting, but all she felt was a strange emptiness. The meticulously decorated spaces looked stark, the polished antiques looked more like museum pieces than the furnishings of a home, and the silence of solitude pressed against her ears.

She shivered, inexplicably chilled.

CHAPTER ELEVEN

FOR the first time she could remember, Frances overslept the next morning, an experience every bit as disconcerting as anything that had happened to her in the last week. She dressed quickly in a brown suit so severely tailored that it was almost masculine, snatched her briefcase and scurried out of the door.

In spite of her haste, she arrived at work a full hour after all the other employees. Incredulous stares followed her as she hurried through the outer office. I'm not *that* late, she thought irritably, uncomfortable under their stares.

Frowning, she walked faster through the honeycombed labyrinth of working cubicles. There were no calls of welcome, no hellos after her absence, and, although she wouldn't have considered that odd a week ago, after the friendliness of the citizens of Nowthen, she found it unsettling. I'm in a room full of people I've worked with for years, she thought morosely, and yet I'm more isolated here than I was in a town of strangers.

And it wasn't just the lack of communication that made her feel so separated from her fellows; she felt oddly dissociated from the frenzied activity around her. Everyone seemed to be hurrying, even if they were sitting still. Dozens of phones jangled, computer keyboards clattered, pencils scurried across paper in a frantic race toward an unseen finishing line.

What are they all *doing*? she wondered, forgetting completely that just a short time ago she had been one of them.

The company president raised his graying head to look at her as she entered his private office.

"Good morning," she said, approaching his desk. "I'm sorry I'm so late..."

He dismissed her apology with an absent wave of his hand, then cocked his head and studied her curiously.

Frances frowned a little, her hands twisting together behind her back. Why was he looking at her like that? Why was everybody looking at her so strangely this morning? Just because she'd been late?

"It's good to have you back, Frances." He paused, then smiled. "I like your hair, by the way."

Her hand moved automatically toward the place where her hair should have been nested in its tight little coil, but then she remembered that she hadn't put it up this morning; she simply hadn't had the time. It had never occurred to her that anyone would notice or think it odd—she'd worn it loose and curled over her shoulders in Nowthen, after all...but you're not in Nowthen any more, she reminded herself sternly. In all the years she'd worked at this office, she'd never once let her hair hang free. No wonder everyone was staring at her this morning; they probably didn't recognize her.

"Sit down, Frances. Make yourself comfortable." The president beamed at her from across the desk. "I had a call from one of your friends this morning."

Frances sifted through the mental file of her friends and found the file dismayingly empty. Her brows twitched in a question.

"From Nowthen," he explained, and her breath caught sharply in her throat.

Ethan. It had to be Ethan, she thought, her knees suddenly weak, her hand groping blindly for the chair behind her. "Really?" she whispered, sinking onto the leather cushion, steeling herself for the sound of his name spoken aloud. She sat on the edge of the seat, her feet close together on the floor, her hands tightly folded in her lap. Her eyes were overly bright, like amber jewels in sunlight.

"It seems you made quite an impression." He smiled. "Elaine Harmon called and asked for your home address..."

The air gradually seeped out of her lungs, as if they were a balloon with a slow, steady leak. Not Ethan, she thought, her features sagging almost imperceptibly.

"... and normally we would never release an employee's address," the president was saying, "but, in the circumstances, I didn't think you'd mind. She said they wanted to send you a gift."

"Oh." Frances smiled weakly. "How nice."

"The Harmons couldn't say enough about you," he prattled on. "About all the friends you made in Nowthen, all the goodwill you generated for Northeastern Casualty while you were there..."

Frances pretended to listen with polite attention, her head cocked, a proper smile fixed on her face, her eyes bright with apparent interest; but the truth was she barely heard a word he said. *Not Ethan,* her thoughts kept repeating senselessly.

After what seemed like a very long time, she heard her name spoken twice as a question, and noticed the president frowning at her with concern. She blinked and forced her eyes to focus on his face.

"Are you all right, Frances?"

She nodded quickly, forcefully. "Of course."

"You seem ... distracted."

"I'm a little tired. It was a long drive yesterday."

He nodded thoughtfully, still frowning at her. "Maybe you should take the rest of the day off..."

"I'm fine," she insisted, her voice a little too bright.

After what seemed like an endless conference on the Paris assignment, she retreated to the privacy of her own office to study the file he had given her, but her gaze kept drifting from the stacks of paperwork on her desk to the view from her window. She noticed things from her tenth-story vantage point she couldn't remember noticing before: the rumble of heavy traffic rising from the street below, the unsettling blandness of a cityscape after the riotous color of the country. It should have been comforting and familiar, this view of the city that had been her home since her birth, but it was neither. She felt like an alien posing as a citizen in some foreign land, a displaced person whose hiding place just hadn't been discovered yet.

There was no comfort to be found in the outer office either. When she emerged for an afternoon break she caught herself staring in bafflement at the other employees as they scurried about, racing up the ladder of success, mindless of whom or what they trampled in their rush to the top. Had she really found such an environment invigorating? she wondered. Had all this senseless competition been the heady potion of life just last week?

It'll be better tomorrow, she kept telling herself.

But it wasn't better the next day, or the next, or even the next. She still felt like an outsider at work, and, although she counted the hours every day until she could leave, arriving home was always a disappointing anticlimax. She felt strangely divided, like a tourist on vacation who longed for the comforting familiarity of home. All the things she had always loved about Boston—its urbane sophistication, its vital nightlife, its culture—seemed blatantly superficial. Even at the long-awaited opening of the Kirov Ballet, Frances caught herself thinking that tonight was the night of the band concert in Nowthen; that she was missing the community picnic.

After she'd been back at work a full week, a secretary brought in her ticket to Paris. "You leave next Wednesday," she said with an envious smile. "I wish it were me."

Frances stared after her. "So do I," she whispered after the girl had left.

On the way home she stopped at a favorite restaurant, sat at her usual table for one, and found it lonely. The excellent food seemed to turn to dust in her mouth, and she left most of it untouched, confused and irritated by her sudden desire for a plate of Margaret's potato salad.

You're being stupid, she scolded herself later, slamming the door of her town house behind her. She scowled at the antique table in the foyer as if it were somehow to blame for her state of mind. It terrified her that thoughts of Nowthen had kept sneaking into her mind all week, disrupting the orderly pattern of her life. What was wrong with her? How could she think of a backward, one-horse town like Nowthen when she had Boston at her feet and Paris waiting? What was so seductive about a plate of potato salad, a little country hospitality, a single afternoon in a hotel bed...?

The force of that memory, the one she had hidden in the furthest corner of her mind, seemed to push her backward against the door. She sagged against it breathlessly, trying to explain away the strange emptiness in the region of her heart; the hollow sensation of something missing.

It's because it's quiet, she decided after a moment. This place is just too damn quiet. Maybe I need a pet. A cat, maybe, or a dog...

But that only reminded her of the growling, frightened dog that bore her name, and that only reminded her of Ethan...

Don't think of him! she commanded herself, her eyes squeezed tightly shut. Think of something else; anything else... her thoughts pulled at the store of her memories, but all they could retrieve was a strong, chiseled face with eyes the color of a peacock's tail...

She straightened abruptly, like a puppet whose strings had *suddenly* been pulled taut. Without giving herself a moment to think about what she was going to do, she marched to the phone, snapped open her address book, and dialed. Her knees almost buckled at the sound of his voice coming over the wire. "Ethan?" she whispered.

"Frannie?"

The words tumbled out of her mouth, as if she'd been holding them all on her tongue in a clump. "I thought maybe you'd like to come down to Boston tomorrow to go out to dinner, and I have tickets for the symphony, or if you'd rather we could——"

"I have to go, Frannie—I'm on my way to an emergency call. I'll be there by noon."

He broke the connection so abruptly that she just stood there for a moment, lips slightly parted, listening to the dial tone. "He's coming," she finally whispered aloud, and then, like a teenage girl anticipating her first date, she scurried to her bedroom to pick out what she would wear. It had to be perfect. Everything had to be perfect.

When the doorbell sounded precisely at noon the next day, Frances froze in front of the bedroom mirror, instantly, inexplicably terrified. She'd been perfectly happy with her appearance up until the moment the bell rang; now, it suddenly looked all wrong.

Her eyes seemed too light, her complexion too pale, her lipstick too dark. Dammit, she thought, worrying her lower lip with her teeth, imagining that the mint green blouse looked cheap, that the V-neck dipped too low and showed too much. Even the softly draped white dress pants managed to look clownlike. It's the hair, she decided, quickly tugging the light reddish-brown mass behind her head, clasping it at the base of her neck with a slide. That seemed to help, and she hurried to answer the second ring of the bell.

When she opened the door they stared at each other for a moment, equally motionless. Ethan was wearing snug, faded jeans with a white shirt open at the collar, exposing a slash of deeply tanned chest that made the shirt look almost iridescent. She thought he looked taller here than he had in Nowthen, as if the city sky hung a little bit lower, almost brushing the white-blond sun-streaks in his hair. She noticed all these things only peripherally, because her eyes never left his. She wondered where the peacock-blue color had gone. Today they looked darker, nearly cobalt.

Nervousness made her greeting sound affected, the kind of cordial graciousness one exhibited to strangers. "Hello, Ethan. Won't you come in?"

He nodded perfunctorily and moved inside. Frances closed the door and leaned against it, smiling tremulously. "You're looking well," she said, but he didn't reply. His lips twitched a bit, as if noting her discomfort, the lameness of her remark.

The seconds ticked by with maddening slowness as he remained silent. Soon Frances felt the strain of her cheek muscles as they struggled to hold a false smile. "Let's have some wine, shall we?" she said brightly, rubbing her hands together, bustling past him into the kitchen. She wasn't even sure she *had* any wine, but she would have made any excuse to escape his silent stare.

As she knelt in front of the open refrigerator she heard the soft squeak of his tennis shoes crossing the tile floor.

"Ah, here we are." With great relief, she pulled an unopened bottle of Chablis from the back of the bottom shelf. Struggling to control the trembling of her hands, she opened the bottle and filled two glasses. She didn't look at him again until they touched glasses, facing each other.

"To your first visit." She tried to make her voice sound light, but her smile faltered under the intensity of his stare. She dropped her gaze instantly, frowning. "Why aren't you saying anything?" she mumbled, confused.

"I don't know what to say."

"Say hello," she blurted out. "Say it's nice to see me again; say *something*!"

He sighed aloud, then said, "You're nervous." It sounded like an accusation.

"Of course I'm nervous." She tried for a light, merry laugh, but it sounded more like a weak gasp. "I've never done this sort of thing before..."

"What sort of thing?"

She shrugged, embarrassed. "You know... called a man for a date..."

His brows shot upward. "A date? Is that what this is?"

Frances took a quick mental step backward, retreating from the undercurrent of anger she heard in his voice.

This isn't going well, she thought, dismayed by the awkwardness she felt. The feeling between them was different here; *he* was different here, as if whatever had drawn them together could exist only within the narrow confines of Nowthen.

"Maybe calling you was a mistake," she mumbled toward the floor.

She glanced up furtively at the sound of his sigh, saw that he had turned his head and was looking around, affecting an interest in the rather boring surroundings of the galley kitchen. "So this is where you live," he said dully. He tipped his glass to his mouth and drained half the contents. Frances watched the muscles of his throat stretch, then constrict as he swallowed. He's too tall for this room, she thought, too broad. Suddenly she felt trapped, almost claustrophobic, as if there wasn't enough oxygen in the small kitchen for both of them.

"Come see the rest," she said breathlessly, walking quickly past him to the dining room, acutely aware of his eyes on her back.

In the living room he moved from place to place, grazing the gleaming surface of her cherished antiques with a light hand as she turned in a circle in the center of the room, watching him. This room was the showcase for her finest pieces—the most beautiful antiques, the most valuable artwork—but somehow watching Ethan move among them seemed to diminish their value. She frowned when he stopped and cocked his head to examine the watercolor that hung over the couch, the only item in the room that was relatively worthless.

"I like it," he pronounced. "Very much. But I don't know the artist." He scowled at the scrawled signature.

"He's just an art student at the university. He doesn't exhibit anywhere. The truth is he was selling that on the sidewalk downtown. I don't know what made me buy it, or hang it, for that matter. It isn't worth anything."

Ethan turned his head slowly to look at her, his eyes quiet. "You bought it because it's beautiful. That makes it worth a great deal." Suddenly his lips lifted in a barely perceptible smile, and Frances felt her heart skip a beat. "Maybe there's hope for you yet, Frannie."

She clasped her hands tightly in front of her and held her breath. He'd called her Frannie, and, for some reason she couldn't begin to explain, that made her want to cry.

"Show me the rest of your place," he said suddenly.

She showed him everything, warming to the task as they moved through the house. She was almost childishly proud of her acquisitions, and without realizing it she began to recite the history and value of each piece as if she were a guide in a gallery.

Ethan was quietly attentive for the most part, but the few comments he did make displayed a surprising knowledge of art. It wasn't until they'd finished the tour and were back in the kitchen that Frances remembered his roots were in wealth, that for all she knew his family probably owned the originals of the prints she hung so proudly.

"Where did you grow up?" she asked him abruptly.

He didn't answer until he'd helped himself to another glass of wine. "Not far from here, actually."

"You're from Boston too?"

He nodded once, irritably, then mentioned an older, gracious neighborhood on the other side of Boston's Charles River; a neighborhood of large properties and stately mansions that Frances had only seen once, from the window of a tour bus.

"Do your parents still live there?"

"I suppose."

"You suppose?" she frowned. "Don't you know?"

Ethan shrugged angrily and looked away. "I haven't talked to them in years. We don't have much in common...I thought Beth told you all this."

"She told me you never talked about your family; she didn't tell me you never talked *to* them..."

"So? What difference does it make?"

Frances's jaw dropped open. "And you had the nerve to lecture me about the importance of relationships? A man who's divorced himself totally from his family, his home——"

"It's *not* my home," he reminded her coldly. Suddenly his gaze seemed to sharpen and focus on her with laserlike intensity. "At least not any more than the neighborhood you came from is *your* home. Maybe you'd like to tell me the last time you visited there?"

"I don't need to visit the old neighborhood to talk to my mother," she countered sharply. "We usually meet somewhere in between. Besides, it's the relationship that matters, not where we relate."

Ethan stared at her for a moment, then shook his head helplessly. "Very profound, Frances," he said wryly. "Too bad you never listen to yourself."

She bristled instinctively at his sarcasm, missing the point entirely. "I've made lunch," she snapped, turning toward the refrigerator. "Sit down."

"No."

She stiffened and turned—and ran right into the wall of his chest. He snatched at her waist before she could react and jerked her against him.

"I don't want to have lunch, Frances." He caught her by the shoulders when she tried to twist away, and the force of his grip was a measure of the anger he was keeping in check. "I want to know what the hell this is all about. Why did you want me to come down here?"

Frances leaned her upper body backward, wincing at the pressure of his fingers digging into the soft flesh of her shoulders. "I just thought it would be nice to see you again, that's all."

He froze suddenly, his face still, his eyes seeming to drain of color as the feeling seeped out of them. "You thought it would be *nice*?" he repeated numbly. "My God, this really is a date, isn't it? That's all you had in mind..."

"What's wrong with that?" she demanded, squirming in his grasp with little effect, frustration rapidly changing to fury. "I was stupid enough to think I wanted to see you again. Is that so terrible?"

She remembered the first time she saw him smile; the way it had seemed to light up the dim alleyway of the barn...but that wasn't the smile he was wearing now. This one was...dark, somehow terrible.

"You thought we'd have a nice little affair, didn't you, Frances?" His voice was terrible too; flat, emotionless. Wary now, she tried to back away, but he jerked her back against him so hard that all the breath left her body in an audible gasp. "You thought you could have it both ways, didn't you? Your own life, and part of mine too, as long as the two didn't get too close. Was that the plan? Is that the ultimate achievement for the modern woman? Life as usual, as long as you have a man periodically to satisfy your need for——"

"No!" she breathed, struggling in earnest now, her hands splayed against his chest, pushing as hard as she could. "I don't know what you're talking about..."

"I'm talking about what you want from me," he growled, then he caught the back of her head and jerked it toward his. He glared down at her for a moment, confirming with his eyes what he did with his mouth a second later.

Frances stiffened in shock as her lips flattened under his, and in that moment of stunned hesitation, his free hand slipped down to her buttocks, tugging them into his hips. While her mind was frantically trying to process this new sensation, his tongue swept across the seam of her lips, opening them.

Fight him! she commanded her body in that last moment of rational thought, but her body's only response was to sag helplessly against him. A tiny moan crawled up her throat at the answering thrust of hardness pressing into her pelvis, and any thought of resistance dissolved.

"Ethan," she breathed into his open mouth, feeling a sharp stab of triumph when he groaned and staggered backward to lean against the counter. A moment ago he had held her captive by virtue of his strength; now, by virtue of her sex, the division of power was equal.

"Is this what you want from me?" he demanded hoarsely, his hands moving to course over the thrusting swell of her breasts.

Whatever words she might have spoken froze in her throat at the insistent press of his hands, and her knees buckled as she started to sink to the floor. Almost instantly he grasped her waist, lifted her effortlessly and turned to set her on the counter, stepping between her legs, breathing hard as his hands fumbled with the buttons of her blouse. "Damn," he muttered once, then ripped the blouse open, sending the buttons flying.

Frances leaned her head back against the upper cabinet and closed her eyes as he buried his face in the valley between her breasts. Swollen and almost painfully sensitive, they pushed against the thin lace of her bra, spilling over the top. He tugged the bra downward to free them, and when his mouth closed over one nipple she gasped aloud, clutched the back of his head and pulled him tightly against her.

"So what's it going to be, Frances?" he murmured, and his breath felt like a firestorm against her skin as his mouth moved down the line between her rib cage to her navel. She never felt his hands opening the front closure of her pants. "Shall we see each other once a month?" he asked, his tongue slipping beneath the lace top of her panties, making her gasp. "Twice? Should I always come down here for sex, or will you come to Nowthen occasionally?"

Frances went rigid and her eyes opened wide.

He straightened until his eyes were on a direct line with hers. Even though she could feel the heat emanating from his body, his eyes were cold, and even though his breathing was rapid and ragged his voice was perfectly controlled. It was a frightening contrast, to see the force of his will commanding the awesome power of passion. "Or shall we keep the two worlds totally separate and just meet somewhere in between," he finished bitterly, "like you do with your mother?"

"Don't," she whispered bleakly. "Don't talk like that...don't make it sound so..."

"Cheap? Casual? What else would you call a sexual relationship without commitment?" He closed his eyes briefly, and when he opened them again they seemed to plead with her. "Come home, Frances. Do it. Commit to something important for once in your life."

She slammed her eyes closed so she wouldn't have to look at him, and her fingertips whitened as she gripped the edge of the counter. "You're not being fair," she whispered, her voice trembling. "This *is* my home. How can you demand that I leave it, when you aren't willing to do as much? You could work in Boston; we could live right here..."

His gaze was unrelenting. "Now why would I want to live here?" he asked quietly. "Frances Katharine Hudson lives here, and I'm not in love with her. I'm in love with a woman called Frannie, and, so far, I've only seen her in Nowthen."

She hesitated for a moment, the woman who was Frannie and the fighter who was Frances struggled for control inside. Her face reflected the battle within, and finally, the victor. "I've worked hard to make a life for myself here," she said at last.

The seconds ticked by as Ethan searched her face. Finally he nodded once, closed his eyes, and released a heavy sigh. Then with the touching gentleness of a parent, rather than a lover, he refastened her pants, eased her bra back over her breasts, and closed her blouse.

Frances sat motionless during the whole procedure, her mind numb. She watched the strands of fair hair quiver on his head as his hands worked, fighting the impulse to reach out and smooth them back. When he was finished he took a step back from the counter and looked at her without expression. She could see her reflection in the shine of his eyes, and thought she looked very small.

"We never really had a chance, did we?" he asked with a sad smile.

She continued to sit motionless on the counter for a long time after he had left.

CHAPTER TWELVE

FOR almost an hour after Ethan had left Frances walked mindlessly through the rooms of her house, her mind steeled against a rising tide of emotions she knew would drown her, given the chance. Eventually she found her way into the bedroom and shed the blouse and pants, letting them crumple into a silk heap on the floor.

Don't think about it, she commanded herself, staring lifelessly at her reflection in the full-length mirror. It was strange to see the rise of her breasts beneath her bra, to remember that just a short while ago his hands and his mouth had been there . . .

She slammed her eyes closed and gritted her teeth. From that moment on she operated on instinct, because thought was the enemy she had to avoid at all costs. It was without thinking, then, that she pulled on the jeans and T-shirt she had bought in Nowthen and brushed her hair into a high ponytail to get it off her neck. And it was without thinking that she grabbed her keys and walked out of the front door and headed toward her car.

It took her less than half an hour to drive from the steel and glass high rises of her present to the squat brick buildings of her past. It was true that she hadn't visited the old neighborhood all that often in the past few years. The last thing she had wanted in her new life was a constant reminder of her old one—and yet today the reminder didn't seem so bad. The narrow streets didn't look quite as dark as she remembered them; the ageing red brick of the buildings looked rosy and warm in the light of the afternoon sun, rather than shabby.

As she pulled her car close to the curb, she wondered if the neighborhood had really changed, or just the way she looked at it. She thought about that as she entered the building that was her mother's home—that had been *her* home for the first eighteen years of her life.

The moment she opened the door the sounds and smells of her youth enveloped her. As she climbed the creaking wooden stairs to the second floor, she breathed in the mingled aromas of memory—Mrs. McFiel was baking her sweet, lemony-scented poppyseed cakes tonight, and in someone else's apartment a pot of spaghetti sauce was simmering on the stove.

Frances smiled without realizing she was smiling, listening to the somehow restful sound of a distant baby's tired fretting, the soft, mellow moan of a saxophone rising from a basement apartment.

She stopped at her mother's door and looked at all the scars in the old wood, letting the past wash over her like the gentle ripples of a warm bath. There had been constant knocking at this door when Frances had been growing up, and there probably still was. Her mother's sweet, generous nature was almost legendary in this part of town, and, although she claimed she was blessed to have so many kind friends and neighbors, the truth was that blessings had nothing to do with it; she had earned every one.

But it wasn't just the kindness of neighbors that kept her mother here—there were kind people everywhere, Frances was learning—it was something else, something she didn't quite understand yet.

"Frannie!" Her mother answered her knock, happy surprise deepening the creases a million smiles had made in her face. Frances returned the smile, looking into the mirror of her own features, seeing eyes shaped like hers, but more warmly colored. The short, softly arranged hair was predominantly gray, but still bore a hint of rich russet. "You haven't been here in so long...what a wonderful surprise!" Her mother hugged her fiercely, then held her at arm's length. "Look at you!" she smiled, her expression a mixture of puzzlement and pleasure. "You look like the old Frannie in that outfit."

Frances frowned down at the jeans and T-shirt as if she'd never seen them before. "I wasn't thinking...I just pulled on whatever was lying around."

Her mother clucked her tongue. "Nothing is ever 'just lying around' at your place, Frannie. Have you eaten lunch yet? Never mind. Even if you have, it wasn't enough—you eat like a bird. Come to the kitchen—we'll have coffee, maybe a little apple pie hot out of the oven, and then we'll make a grand supper for the two of us..."

Frances looked after her, smiling helplessly. It wouldn't do any good to refuse coffee or pie or a ten-course meal if that was what her mother wanted her to have. The nurturing instinct was as strong now as it had been when Frances was a little girl.

She followed slowly, passing through a living room crammed with gifts she had given her mother over the years—modern, expensive gifts that for some reason looked out of place today, like snatches of an alien future caught in the time-warp of the tiny, old-fashioned apartment. She scowled at the glaring incongruity of a pricy abstract print hanging on the faded floral wallpaper her mother refused to tear down. And then there was that tattered, cheap silk scarf draped over the crisp lines of a large-screen television. Couldn't her mother see how awful that looked? And couldn't she see the sheer silliness of the brand-new computerized sewing machine sitting on top of that battered old treadle model she refused to throw away, just because it had been a gift from——

Frances caught her breath and stopped in the middle of the room, her eyes as busy as her body was motionless. Dear Lord! Everywhere she looked. The man had been dead for over a quarter of a century, and yet here he was, everywhere she looked—in the old sewing machine, in the garish print of that aging scarf he'd given her mother nearly three decades before; even in the wallpaper he had hung and smoothed with his own hands the year they were married...

She released the breath she had been holding and closed her eyes, feeling utterly overwhelmed by both the presence and the absence of a man she had never really known. When she opened her eyes again they went automatically to the yellowed, wrinkled black and white photograph of her father, smiling eternally from its permanent place of honor on the table next to her mother's easy chair. "It's you," she whispered at the stranger in the picture, feeling a traitorous prickle behind her eyes. "It's you that she can't bear to leave behind..."

"Coming, Frannie?"

She started at her mother's voice, blinked rapidly, then took a deep breath before moving toward the kitchen. She stopped in the doorway and looked at her mother, sitting at the chipped Formica table, knife poised over the golden crust of a steaming pie. Behind her were the decorative oak cabinets her father had carved; beneath her feet was the scuffed linoleum that had once been bright and new, chosen and laid by an excited bride and her new husband.

"Why didn't you ever tell me?" she whispered from the doorway.

Her mother looked over at her, her brows cocked curiously over warm, dark eyes. "Why didn't I ever tell you what, honey?"

"The real reason you wouldn't leave this place."

"But I have told you, a hundred times at least, Frannie," her mother said gently. "This is my home."

Frances pressed her lips tightly together and shook her head. "It's because Father's here, isn't it? That's the real reason."

Her mother's hand stilled in the motion of slicing the pie. "He's the reason it *is* home, Frannie," she said quietly, and suddenly Frances felt like crying because she had never understood that before.

"I should never have asked you to leave here," she managed to choke out. "I should have known, I should have understood..."

"Frannie!" Her mother raised her head with that smile Frances had seen a thousand times growing up; the smile that said it didn't matter if you broke the good vase or spilled your milk or ripped your best Sunday dress on the playground. Love forgave everything. "You were too young when he died. You never knew me as a woman in love, only as a mother. You couldn't

possibly have understood that what your father and I had together is all tied up with this place..."
She paused and cocked her head, studying her daughter's face, frowning and smiling at the same time. "But if you understand now, I think maybe you'd better tell me what happened to you in New Hampshire, don't you?"

Their eyes locked for a moment, spanning the distance between their two worlds, between the two sets of values that had been so vastly different for so long. What Frances saw in her mother's face—the greatness of a love that could span the decades and defeat even death—took her breath away. Did her own face look like that when she thought of Ethan? And if it did, could there be anything in the world more important than that? Any achievement greater than committing totally to that kind of love? In that moment, Frances was certain that if she reached up she would feel pigtails on either side of her head.

She walked to the table and sat down, suddenly in awe of her own mother; of the woman who had always understood that home wasn't the city you lived in or the job you worked at or even the man-made walls that surrounded the symbols of your achievement.

The real sense of home began with the love between a man and a woman, a love so strong that it put down roots wherever it was planted— in a city high rise, in an old, poor neighborhood like this one... maybe even in a remote farming town like Nowthen.

Frannie smiled a little at that, and then she began to talk.

It was after midnight by the time she left her mother's. They'd talked until they were both nearly hoarse, trying to make up in one night all the years of communicating they'd missed, when neither had understood the other. They had laughed at Frannie's stories of Nowthen, at the mental picture she painted of the staid city businesswoman kneeling in a barn; they'd cried at the stories about her father she'd never heard before; and, through it all, they began to relate not only as mother and daughter, but as two women who both knew what it was to love a man.

A light drizzle was washing the city air as Frances started her car and pulled away from the curb. Traffic lights winked merrily over the deserted streets, their greens and yellows and reds reflecting on the wet pavement below. As she drove from the old neighborhood toward the glittering towers of uptown that had so entranced her as a child, Frances thought she had never seen the grand old city looking so beautiful.

I'm going to miss it, she thought suddenly, and it was only in that moment that the full impact of her decision hit her. She would leave the only place she had ever called home; the career she had struggled for years to develop; the house she had cherished as the symbol of her worth. "Well, Frances Katharine Hudson," she murmured in quiet amazement, "what a surprising choice you've made!" She glanced into the car's rear-view mirror, saw a fresh-faced, ponytailed young woman staring back at her and smiled. Frances Katharine Hudson hadn't made the choice at all; Frannie had.

"Frannie." She said the name aloud, loving the sound of it, wondering why she hadn't always loved the sound of it. The people who really knew her, the people who loved her, always called her Frannie—people like her mother; people like Ethan.

Just forming his name in her mind made her press a little harder on the accelerator. I'll call him, she determined, speeding through the warren of downtown streets, barely noticing the towers that had been the focus of her life for so long. I'll call him and tell him . . .

Tell him what? She puzzled over that for a while, brow furrowed, lips pursed, heart beating in time to the steady thump of the windshield wipers; then she decided. She'd tell him she was coming home.

She had left the house without turning on the outside lights, and tripped twice on the wet front walk in her hurry to get inside and place her call. The night was filled with the music of the rain, the gentle patter of raindrops on leaves, the muted plopping of those drops as they found the puddles beneath...but then there was a sound that didn't belong; a rustle from the shadows of her doorway. Frances froze in place as adrenalin shot into her veins. One of the shadows by the door separated from the others, rising to an enormous, terrifying height.

"Frannie?" the shadow called out quietly.

"Ethan?" she whispered, her heart still hammering.

He took a step out of the doorway and the filtered light from a distant street lamp struck the lightest strands of his fair hair.

"Ethan!" she breathed, taking in the rain-soaked shirt clinging to his chest, the thick, beautiful hair now plastered wetly to skull and forehead. She moved toward him, murmuring, "Good Lord, look at you..."

She didn't have a chance to say anything else. He swept her into his arms and pulled her close, burying his face in her neck, speaking her name against her skin—her *real* name. The keys fell from her hand as she wrapped her arms around his neck and clung to him, quivering.

"Dammit, where were you?" he growled just beneath her ear, trying to sound stern but failing miserably. "When I came back and you were gone..."

Frannie smiled and pushed away just far enough to look up into his eyes. They were brilliantly blue again. "I went to see my mother."

He opened his mouth in a silent laugh. "So did I. You shamed me into it, with that crack about me having no right to preach to you about relationships when I'd divorced myself from my family..." He hesitated, smiling down at her tenderly. "We've both wasted a lot of time running from where we started, haven't we, Frannie? Trouble is, when you run away from places, you leave people behind too and some of them don't deserve that. My mother, for one."

"And mine," Frannie whispered.

For a moment they stood in the circle of each other's arms, reading the love they saw in each other's eyes, oblivious to the rain pelting down on their heads and shoulders and arms, soaking through their clothes.

"I'm moving back to Boston, Frannie," he whispered at last, and, when she opened her mouth to make a surprised protest, he covered her lips with one finger. "I didn't even have to think about it—not really. The day you left I knew I didn't belong in Nowthen any more."

Frances moved her lips against his finger, smiling when he caught his breath. "I see," she murmured. "So you're moving to Boston..."

"That's right."

She tipped her head and smiled at him with a touch of mischief. "Well then, maybe you're in the market for a nice town house? Fully furnished, beautifully decorated...of course, the style is a bit austere for my tastes, but——"

He grabbed her shoulders and bent his knees to bring his eyes on a level with hers. "What are you talking about?"

She feigned innocence. "I'm talking about a terrific real estate opportunity," she insisted. "It would never have come on the market at all, if the lady who owns it hadn't taken a trip north..." she touched a finger to the corner of his mouth, "...met a man..." she was whispering now, watching with rapt fascination as his lips caught the tip of her finger and pulled it into his mouth, "...and fallen so hopelessly in love that..." she caught her breath when his hands slid down to cup her buttocks and pull her gently against him, "...and the thing is..." His hips moved against hers, and she used the last of her breath to murmur, "Now she can't wait to get back home..."

Ethan's breathing was ragged, his eyes so intensely alight that Frannie thought she might catch fire if she looked at them too long. "I'm not easy, you know," he said hoarsely, a smile playing at the corners of his mouth. "You're going to have to promise to marry me to get me into bed." His hands slid under her T-shirt and up to her breasts, and her words came out in a rush of air.

"I promise," she whispered.

CHAPTER THIRTEEN

"WHERE are we going?" Frannie asked Ethan as they headed away from the church. They were pressed close together in the velvet-covered seat of a fringe-topped surrey, drawn by two prancing white horses. Frannie thought the steady clop-clop of their hoofs sounded remarkably, appropriately, like the happy beating of two hearts.

"To our reception, of course," Ethan smiled. He wore a dark suit with a brilliantly white shirt and a black string tie, the traditional wedding garb of a much younger America. Frannie wore a full-skirted, old-fashioned eyelet dress with a scoop neck and short puffy sleeves.

"Reception?" she asked, reaching up to adjust the wide brim of her tulle hat, touching the tiny clusters of baby's breath threaded into the band. "I thought we weren't having a reception..."

Ethan clucked gently at the horse and grinned. "That's what everybody wanted you to think. The whole town's been working on this for nearly a month. Elaine and Margaret started the ball rolling, but pretty soon everybody pitched in, making plans, getting things ready. They wanted to surprise you. Take a look." He pointed to the park entrance just ahead.

The wrought-iron arch was festooned with white silk ribbon and clusters of daisies. Across the top, a wide banner declared "Good Luck, Frannie and Ethan!"

As the surrey passed under the entry arch, a cheer rose from the waiting crowd. There were dear, familiar faces in that crowd—Elaine's and Franklin's, Margaret's, Beth's—but somehow Frannie knew that even the unfamiliar faces would become dear soon enough. She had finally come home. As the Nowthen Senior Citizens' Band began a rousing rendition of the "Wedding March" in the distant bandstand, Frannie pressed her lips together and felt her eyes begin to fill. "I love this town," she whispered. Ethan pulled her more tightly into the circle of his arm.

The next few hours passed in a mindless, euphoric blur. Frannie vaguely remembered floating around a wooden floor in front of the bandstand, Ethan's arm snugged around her waist, his lips pressed to her ear.

After that first dance there was a seemingly endless series of well-scrubbed, freshly shaven men's faces bobbing over hers, stammering good wishes as earnest as their expressions. She was hugged by strangers, kissed by people she barely knew, taken into innumerable unfamiliar arms, and all of it seemed absolutely, perfectly right.

Finally Ethan and Frannie ceased to be the focus of the celebration, and were free to sit quietly on the very bench they had first shared in this park, hands intertwined, heads close together.

"Look at that," she whispered, her eyes brightly focused on a nearby table where her mother and Miles were engaged in earnest, almost intimate conversation. Something Miles said made her mother tip her head sideways and laugh softly, almost coquettishly, and Frannie felt a strange, happy warmth course through her body. She nudged Ethan, and, when he didn't respond, cocked her head to peer up at his face. He was staring with mystified amazement at his stuffy, proper father, tie loosened, spinning his wife around the floor in a vigorous polka.

Frannie smiled serenely at the unlikely scene, not at all surprised. Boston's high-minded propriety died a sudden, pleasant death in this town. No one knew that better than she did.

Later, happily tangled in the twisted sheets, propped on one elbow, Frannie watched her husband sleep in the golden glow of a bedside lamp. She marveled quietly at the sheer beauty of his features in repose, at the extraordinary sense of fulfilment making love with him could bring...especially when she was so sure...

She smiled and rolled onto her back, spreading her fingers across her lower stomach, somehow sensing that the love they had shared this particular night was too vast to be limited by the act that demonstrated it. Her smile softened with a sigh as she pressed gently with her fingers, a mother's first greeting to the life beginning beneath her hands.

"Frannie?" Ethan murmured, suddenly, fully awake. He rolled onto his side and covered her hand with his.

"Can you feel it, Ethan?" she whispered, her eyes wide with wonder to be finally making her mark on the world.

HARLEQUIN PRESENTS®

A Year
DOWN UNDER

In 1993, Harlequin Presents celebrates the land down under. In April, let us take you to Queensland, Australia, in A DANGEROUS LOVER by Lindsay Armstrong, Harlequin Presents #1546.

Verity Wood usually manages her temperamental boss, Brad Morris, with a fair amount of success. At least she *had* until Brad decides to change the rules of their relationship. But Verity's a widow with a small child—the last thing she needs, or wants, is a dangerous lover!

Share the adventure—and the romance—
of A Year Down Under!

Available this month in
A YEAR DOWN UNDER

THE GOLDEN MASK
by Robyn Donald
Harlequin Presents #1537
Wherever Harlequin books are sold.

YDU-M

Where do you find hot Texas nights, smooth Texas charm and dangerously sexy cowboys?

COWBOYS AND CABERNET

Raise a glass—Texas style!

Tyler McKinney is out to prove a Texas ranch is the perfect place for a vineyard. Vintner Ruth Holden thinks Tyler is too stubborn, too impatient, too...Texas. And far too difficult to resist!

CRYSTAL CREEK reverberates with the exciting rhythm of Texas. Each story features the rugged individuals who live and love in the Lone Star State. And each one ends with the same invitation...

Y'ALL COME BACK...REAL SOON!

Don't miss *COWBOYS AND CABERNET* by Margot Dalton. Available in April wherever Harlequin books are sold.